CONSTELIS VOSS VOL. 1:
COLOUR THEORY

CONSTELIS VOSS VOL. 1: COLOUR THEORY

K. LEIGH

k. LEIGH

Editing by Madalyn Rupprecht
Book design by L. Austen Johnson
Editing and formatting facilitated by Dr. Rissy's Writing & Marketing
Cover Art by Kira Leigh Maintanis

ISBN: 978-1-7368053-0-5 (paperback)
ASIN: B08X7KN68L (ebook)

https://constelisvoss.ml

k. LEIGH

CONTENTS

Content Warning

The following story contains abuse, trauma, PTSD, sexual assault, bigotry, and explicit violence. It is not a piece of fiction that engenders contemporary realities gently, including marginalized identities such as sex workers, LGBTQIAA+ individuals, and people of color.

Please consider this your warning for a work of fiction that exists as a metacritique of the politics of power told through a space opera through one vector of a reality-painted dystopic.

I ask only one thing of you, should you find yourself skimming its pages—enter this self-aware living landscape and question everything.

I hope it teaches who it must, and comforts those I wish to reach. I aim to let my readers know I see them in all their complicated inner paintings.

Good luck, and know that I love you desperately.

"The strategies of the politics of the image has to take a very different and much less guaranteed route, in my view. It has to go *inside* the image itself – inside the image – because stereotypes themselves are really actually very complex things. It has somehow to occupy the very terrain which has been saturated by fixed and closed representation and to try to use the stereotypes and turn the stereotypes in a sense against themselves."

— STUART HALL, "Representation and the Media," Media Education Foundation, 1997

God, it must be lovely being a pretty, wine-mouthed little thing, if only for the hell of it.

I remember when even that was tied to a primary job function; armor in metal bangles, in velvets, in reds, in indigo, only to be made into nothing, and then to unmake someone else.

The paint was my favorite part, but it was always removed in the gnashing of teeth. A smear like the blood on my hands after the job was done.

The lipstick was always red because it's a trick for men.

I'd rather have worn black, but dark colors send the wrong signals. Pretty wine-mouthed little things always paint their roses red, and so too, did I.

These traits are certainly boorish stereotypes, and yet, they *are* stereotypes certain men seek. Certain men who were certain marks, that certainly sought me, that I certainly killed.

It's easier to pull off than you may think, biology notwithstanding.

Especially if you're curiously beautiful, shorter than some, and know how to move like prey animal.

But I was not, and will never be a prey animal.

I am a predator in specific geometry, just like before, just like the rose painted lips, and the smear, and the blood on my hands.

The space between the trick and the repeat job function, too, will be the same.

An evaporation in black waters because time never moves forward. The play is never truly different. We all come together at different acts, but it's always the same because I wrote the script that way.

I wrote it that way because I lived it. And because I lived it, this is my fault.

I'm still the villain with my mouth full of blood, smiling crimson at the mess I established by merit of existing and solved, in black this time. It will be black.

Before that, it will be faux indigo.

We always start with an absence of light, and therefore, color. Then, there's yellow, and at some point, the gold rushes in—not so subtly—until we stretch from hue to hue, get stuck repeatedly on pink, and maybe…

Maybe this time, true indigo will stick instead of black. I haven't decided.

I haven't decided the order in which we all die. Or if we die at all.

It may not even be up to me.

Even if the play is the same, the actors might forget their lines and torch the script with actual fire.

Truth be told, I'm counting on them to do just that.

Because all their fucking lives depend on it.

THE PLAY'S credits performed in reverse. Laughter woven in spliced tongues. Sobs were shots of vodka mimed backward in still-frame memories. Today was the day he was born.

At first, there was a void of nothing. Then, the man was alive. He was alive, standing in a space that smelled like antiseptic. The room was large enough for a swept arm to feel no chairs, no walls, no people, and he was blind.

The tremor of a frenetic pulse in his ears was the beat of a song he knew too well; fight or flight, do or die, the time is *now*.

Then, the sound became a sizzle.

Naturally stumbling, the man placed his hand on a flat surface and followed it up with searching fingers.

He was a slip of a shape, crawling like a bottom-feeder until he reached a notch. He pushed his hand up between the space he felt and grasped what he imagined was silver.

That white-knuckled hand meant he was alive.

He used the handhold to follow the wall and found a seam. He felt the seam with his fingers and plastered his face to a slick surface, his mouth fogging the space in front of him. It was wet on the skin of his cheek.

Finally, after what felt like hours, words found shape in his mouth. If he could speak, it surely meant that he was alive.

"W-where the *fuck* am I?!" he spat against the slick surface near his mouth.

"We had a problem booting you," spoke a muddy voice.

"…booting?" the man replied, voice foreign in his ears.

"We're sanitizing you. We're unsure if contaminants infiltrated your system, so we are making sure there's nothing…wrong. Ok?"

"….no. Not ok. Why the fuck can't I see?" the man asked as the panel shifted away from him with a soft hiss. He fell, fawn-legged, into someone taller than he.

They were a girl, he assumed perhaps foolishly, as his head had connected with their chest. He could smell soft perfume and hear a click, not unlike hooves. He remembered that sound.

"You're talking about me like I'm—I don't fucking know...some kind of Star Trek bullshit..." he blurted out, pushing away from the woman he was braced against.

She caught him and held him to her body. She was breathing, she had a heartbeat, and she smelled like lavender.

"…I had to pull an emergency protocol," she replied as she held him as if he might shatter in her arms.

"Fucking pardon?" he blurted out.

"…you're the last one there is. I had to remove something —a block," the woman said in nothing-words, "I also had to add something in," she admitted with more nothing-words, "though I'm not sure how much it will grow."

"What the fuck does that mean?"

She sat the man down on a lifeless stool after much cajoling. His skin told him that it should be cold, but he felt vaguely anesthetized. He shivered anyways.

"You aren't supposed to be able to shiver…" she said.

"Am I supposed to be able to see, too?" he snapped.

"Sorry about that."

Her heels clicked as she pressed something into the back of his neck. The pressure pulsed up through his jaw into his teeth. His senses screamed into being, birthed in violent indigo.

"Better?" she asked as he heard her step back, the telltale clicking sound grounding him in the here and now.

The man's eyes adjusted, pupils dilating and shrinking in time. The cold white room was bright enough to burn his retinas if he stared long enough.

"Yes," he said, popping his jaw to release the pent-up pressure. It sizzled.

He looked around the blurry room. The metal he had clung to wasn't silver but an unassuming white. Clear glass tables and matching displays filled the room.

All was painted in pales and glass, except for a little green plant in a geometric gold pot—a familiar shape—situated on a far desk. Something lived in a place that seemed so sterile it thwarted all biology.

He looked at the girl before him, as tall as he was but with heels—far taller. A searing blue gaze swept her face; flaccid blond hair, crepe-paper pale skin, with an expression just as brittle. Her lab coat was, however, noticeably tinted.

It was so faint the human eye would ignore the detail. It was hard for him not to notice.

At the far end of the room, a swath of lab coats hung like

bodies on a line. All the color had been bled from the fabric. Her shoes, however, were the color of riches.

"Gold," he said, his mouth impossibly dry.

"Yes. Gold," the woman replied.

"…the plant's yours too, then?" he asked.

"Yes."

The woman looked down at him with large, deep-set brown eyes. The painting of her skin had been covered in makeup, yet the spies of imperfections remained.

She grasped a clear clipboard at her high waist and was fiddling with what looked to be a pen.

"You…don't seem to fit in here. With…all this," the man muttered, accompanied by a vague gesture, "what a weird fucking dream…"

"A120-P, I need you to work with me here," she huffed. Her long fingers tapped on the clipboard.

"…that's not my name," he replied bluntly.

"Then, tell me, smart-ass…what is your name?"

The moment she insulted him, the man's vision flickered to black. Colors hummed behind his eyelids as he squinted to force himself to focus through the mire and the pitch.

A face came into view; the woman he'd fallen into moments earlier. Her rectangular face, her sitting across from him, her eating noodles, her loud slurping; this, he saw, and felt, and smelled.

"You're such a smart-ass, or whatever. You bought, like, two bowls for yourself, and you knew I was on a diet, and you knew you weren't going to eat the other one…"

She still ate despite complaints, twirling her chopsticks to whisk a clump of thick noodles into her bright magenta mouth.

He smelled the food. God, it smelled good…where were they? His thoughts raced, but no answers came.

"Al. Alex. Hey, are you, like...OK?" asked the woman.

"Yeah, Percy. I'm fine. Just thinking about…"

"You need to, like, get over it already. What's done is done."

A pair of fingers snapped the man back to the present. Gone were the slurped noodles. Gone was the banter. Gone was the quaint, slice of life moment from a time that had slipped through his fingers.

The woman before him was an impatient teacher, and he, a young student who was failing her lesson.

"What were you doing? Where did you go? My readings flat-lined…"

"I'm…Alex," he parroted back the name he'd been called in this dream within a dream.

"And where did you go? Come on, you stupid hunk of metal, I am going to be late for my meeting," she insisted.

"…a restaurant? Alright. I'm ready to wake up now. Sci-fi is something Olive likes, so if she tried to use her pixie magic on me, I want the fuck out…" he joked, looking at 'Percy', expecting a caustic retort.

"...who?" the woman asked, arching her brow.

"…Olive?" he insisted.

Alex eagerly awaited Percy's rebuttal, her joke, her smile. The laugh he knew she had that creased at the eyes and showed her too-large teeth.

"No, sweetie…no…" the shrapnel of her words stopped his breathing.

Had he even been breathing?

The tall girl bit her lip. In that instant, colorful shapes, lines, and text clouded his vision. Her heart rate had increased; the numbers leaped.

When she shifted, he saw her weight dispersal; he saw her physical stats, her rank, and her permissions. His sensors painted his vision with the overflowing, fluorescent geometry of...*her*.

He didn't remember ever seeing shit like this before.

Then again, he didn't even remember what 'before' was, either. All he knew was that he was alive, he had been someplace else, and where he was now, wasn't it.

"....so...this isn't a dream?" he asked.

"No," she replied, his vision lighting up with superfluous data the more she moved.

"And, I'm...not a human," he asked.

"No."

"And...I don't know you..." Alex continued, screwing his eyes shut as her data was exploding all around him.

"I'm your technician," the woman insisted, looking over his face.

"But you look like Percy," he argued, eyes flicking open.

"...that's one of the girls from your memory? Like Olive?" she asked.

"Yeah."

The man sat forward and combed his fingers through his hair.

"I have to be fucking dreaming...are you sure we're not knocked out back at Olive's flat, and you're not snoring like a chainsaw?" the weight of his words slumped his shoulders.

"That's why they assigned me. They were trying to be kind—it's an adjustment," she replied with the tap of her pen, "I don't even work in this department."

"They?" he asked, looking up beneath his brows.

"Your…" Not-Percy fidgeted on her heels and tapped her pen again. The metronome of sharp sounds cut his ears.

"Employers. Coworkers…I don't know. I just do what they tell me to," she admitted.

The man smirked, a coy smile playing at the corner of his mouth. His eyes searched her face looking for the girl he'd known.

"God, you even sound like her," he marveled at the painted sunrise of her features. She didn't marvel back.

"I do? I do. Don't I?" she replied.

"What…what's your name?" he hesitated; he already knew her name because her data was blocking his view at the moment.

"Andra. Andra Polly Verdane."

"Polly it is then," he'd decided with a smirk.

"What? No. Andra…" she protested, but it was a feeble effort.

The silence fell thick, with the man smiling and the woman frowning. As he smiled, he focused enough to cut some of the garbage data he saw out of his line of sight. As she frowned further, he managed to store it away altogether.

"Polly, can you get me some fucking pants?"

"It's An—fine," she relinquished her bickering with an eye-roll strong enough to throw planets out of orbit.

Her gold heels clicked like daggers as she walked. She grabbed a pair of standard-issue colorless pants from a drawer and tossed them his way.

A120-P stood and looked down. He was anatomically correct. This, of course, made him snort. Polly wasn't at all amused.

"Hurry up! I'm going to be late!" she spat.

He pulled them on and fastened them with a sticking sound. There was no zipper, and that idea alone made him uneasy.

"Polly?" he asked, fiddling with the strap of his curiously fashioned, colorless pants.

"Yes, A1...Alex?"

"What...do I do here? Why am I...I don't really get it just yet."

"It's expected. You're adjusting," her words sounded as sharp as her heels to the man.

"How...what year is it?" he posed a question for this bright nightmare.

"5352...What year do you last remember?" Polly replied, shifting to favor her right leg.

"1980 or 90 something...at least I think so?" his words were fragile nothing-sounds.

"Oh."

Polly's eyes fell, and her heart rate elevated; he saw the read-out. She grabbed a shirt from a drawer near her knees and tossed it to Alex. He put it on, catching a stab of his face reflecting in a clear display.

He sprinted to the reflection, jostled the table with his hip, and lurched to see himself.

Alex twisted his hair, examined his ears, his jawline, and the curve of his neck with frantic fingers trembling at the foreign canvas.

"...I.." his words were drowned in thick, acidic solvents.

"Do you think you're malfunctioning?" she asked.

"I—what?" he stuttered out, head snapping to attention.

"D-do you feel very distressed? Distressed enough to... do something?"

She tapped her pen rhythmically on her clipboard and stepped back on one high heel. Click.

"N…no. Why? Why would you ask that?" Click.

"Well," Polly's large eyes rolled to the right as she stared at a crease in the floor for a bit too long, "That's why…"

She shot him a look and held his gaze. After a moment, her eyes screwed shut. They opened as she spoke once more.

"That's why you're the only one left."

THE STARS outside were brighter than they should've been.

He was used to being on Earth and seeing the stars tinted darkly by distance. He was used to seeing the sky while standing on that tiny blue and green sphere he remembered. That little blue and green sphere held down by gravity and a molten core. The most constant force in nature had curled around that planet and kept it stuck and starstruck, submitted in the mire of pitch and dark and star.

He was now also starstruck, staring out a small porthole from the assumed laboratory that allowed him to gaze at the nebula they were closest to. He felt bound to look.

Fingers tapped the glass table he was sitting on. His legs were curled with his back flush. He had never been this flexible—this body was better. Yet it wasn't his.

His own ghost was tender to the difference of this shell. Possessing it, but not owning the blue blood in his veins. Nothing, except for Polly, was familiar.

As far as he could assume, the inside of their unfamiliar ship was all white and glass, just like this room. However, it was vast. This he knew.

Constelis Voss was planet-sized.

It was a craft with its own gravitational pull yet could too easily be swept up into a stronger planet's range of influence. His own cornflower blue moon had been tethered to the planet of before, his planet—he remembered. He missed the blue of it.

He thought about the oceans and how they moved. He missed the salt air, the sunny skies, the time spent on rooftops.

Everything he remembered and had known played out in degraded video files. Gaps were filled in by senses he remembered feeling strongly. A scent here, a temperature there, each magnetizing him to a place his ghost begged memory of.

The nebula moved and stole his focus. He could see it shift in small ways, bits of stardust and debris hovering in shards of light. Polly could not see it.

He wondered about it and wondered about the other androids on the ship. He wondered if they felt, or if they had dreams, or even wondered about anything at all.

Would they find beauty in the red stain of the nebula nearest them? Would they think about what it meant to be alive in a time where that nebula was so close, close enough to touch and push through with their own—his own—trembling hands?

Were they even alive? Was he?

The nebula's red sea cast tiny spots of color out into the edges in purple and blue. The center was an eye of black with small medallions of planets hanging like a child's toy. Set high above were strings unseen.

The planets were gravity's puppet, circling a central star that was lemon yellow.

"That's the Fortunus Nebula. It has one habitable planet..." Polly had told him, and nothing more.

He had never seen a sky so full of stars.

Being an android had its perks, he would admit, but there were downsides; if something is too good to be true, it probably is.

Alex dug his fingernails into the skin of his wrist to test a theory. The theory found purchase; the half-moon shapes were imprints of remembered pain not unlike sympathy. He remembered, and so, it hurt.

It felt wrong.

The technician took a reading, as she had every day for the past few weeks, and he said nothing of note. Her large brown eyes stared, butterflied lashes downshifting to look at her clear note terminal, then up again to him, to search his face, to plug something in and out again, then somewhere else, again, and again.

He spoke, willing the words to drip from his mouth.

"....Polly," her name, for the first time, was sharp.

"Yes?"

"...can we go outside?" he asked, holding his marked wrist loosely in his other hand.

"Like, out into space?" she asked.

"No...no." Alex shifted slightly and moved the marked limb to mask his fingers to his face. He peered from beyond them as if in hiding.

"Out of here. I am tired of all the fucking glass and white shit..."

Polly sucked her teeth and stood back on her heels. She had come in, every single day, and every day he had not been allowed to leave. Every day she had run tests, and every day she had asked him about his life before, and every day he had said nothing.

"I'm not supposed to take you out yet. The readings...are concerning."

"...I'm a concern?" he asked, flicking his gaze to her face.

"Yeah—yes. You were the Director's Second, and if you aren't operating optimally, he's not going to want you to continue..."

"Functioning," he finished her sentence with a calculated tilt of his head.

"Yes...that."

"Let me see your notepad, or whatever the fuck it is," he asked.

Polly handed it to him and crossed her arms. He pulled a pitch-black cord from the back of his neck and snapped into the port.

"I'm not supposed to let you d—"

"You have...a network," he mused with a muted smile. This had been the stuff of dreams where he'd come from— when he'd come from. Yet here it was, perfected more than anyone could've ever imagined.

"Of course, we have a—" Alex cut her off with a short sentence.

"I'm downloading a blank OS."

"You don't know how to install it," she protested.

"...yes I do. And I'm not going to overwrite myself. I'm just going to split up fruits in a basket and run off the other one when I need it." Polly was unconvinced.

"...what's this?" his voice was as flat as his expression.

"It's a firewall. You can't be allowed to pop around where you want."

"Of course."

Alex futzed for a few moments as his eyes scanned

nothing she could see. The transparent pad flickered. He copied the video of simply observing data and opened it with a small flash across the screen. She said nothing, and he assumed she did not notice.

She did not notice as he mulled over the firewalls and tried to find a weak point. He didn't manage to crack through, but he remembered where he gravitated towards and what seemed to beg his curiosity. He would try later.

He would try every day for the next week.

Until she was finally cleared to set him loose from his laboratory/prison.

But first, there would be an inspection.

Elsewhere, down in the desecrated bowels of Constelis Voss, Maya had been working on her project for a straight month without stopping.

She had barely slept, not that sleeping ever stopped the fatigue for people like her. She and her peers were perpetually overtaxed; poverty is expensive and exhausting.

Maya swept her matted hair back with her dirty little fingers. She was nearly there, but she lacked the part she needed.

She had spent her entire life working on making something to purify water and make food out of nothing. She dreamed it could be true, and so it must be true.

She stole books. She risked her life in places she didn't belong to learn what could make her dreams real. Not everyone had to try so hard for access to knowledge, and this she knew.

Where she was born and who she was not made all the difference in the world.

Here she was, with all the parts, and was missing just one piece. A basic power core. The most basic of power cores. They were a dime a dozen up there, and yet she didn't have it.

"Fuck!" Maya screwed up her tiny freckled face and slammed her fists on the table beside the project. A few nuts and bolts clattering in a meteor shower to the grates below.

She sat for a moment and turned her head slightly, staring at doubtful thoughts. A long time passed as she clenched and unclenched her fists to an unseen beat.

Tiny bursts of feeling bled through in intervals. Abject despair. Anger. Ironic joy—the kind that comes from being so overwhelmed, one turns acidic.

She hid her emotions. She darted her hand into her pocket to find dirty crumbs to chew. Not enough. Nothing was ever enough in a place where nothings lived and were given nothing.

"Hopeless…" she mumbled to herself, eyes searching beyond what she saw. Her dreams seemed so very far away; beyond, beyond, beyond the stars.

"What if I linked a few together?" she asked herself. A momentary hope, shortly dashed to the rocks. Maya folded over her project as tears threatened that distant, foggy dream.

"I'm…I can't do this anymore…" Maya said to no one.

Not that anyone was listening. They were mostly listening to the sounds of the cosmos, strung out on the copycat designer drugs, laying in the bowels of the shit-stained underbelly of this gigantic, planet-sized vessel.

After using enough, they'd eventually become lifeless vegetables, stop eating, sleeping, cleaning themselves, and breathing altogether. They'd die of apathy staring at the lives of the affluent and fabulous. They'd take in a feed of dreams until they had nothing left.

Maya rubbed snot and tears over her dirty face, her large almond-shaped eyes still glassy. She looked at a poster of a forgotten hero on the wall and pressed a hand to it.

She had found a poster, preserved in shielding, and stole it. Stealing was a heavy word to use when the rules only applied to nothing-people.

Maya traced the outline of the woman's cheek with her finger, trailing up to her dark, cropped haircut, and then to her dismantled torso. Her tiny finger led the charge, outlining a dream made of ink and lines. This was a hero, she felt. The woman's pose said as much.

"...feels hopeless," Maya stammered out, "but you wouldn't let it slow ya' down, right?"

The woman on her ancient poster would never respond to her, but if she could, perhaps she'd agree. Perhaps whatever was keeping it safe would agree; some God in the machine of this hellhole. A flight of fancy, that. It was merely a science.

Maya pulled back from the poster and turned to face the project she toiled over. It was always something to add a spark to a life lived desperately for nothing-people.

Tool in hand, a bright beam of blue flickered on as she worked in the heat, exposed to the elements. She worked with cuts, burns, bruises, and all things terrible lining her fingers and arms.

The metal whined as she rolled her lower lip into her mouth, focused.

The hero she had stolen wouldn't have given up.

Neither could Maya.

THE INSPECTION WAS NOT a glamorous thing. Alex had every port and plug snapped into and jacked up. He looked like a human Christmas tree. Not that anyone here in cosmic utopian la-la land had any idea what Christmas was.

The joke about Christmas he was planning died in his mouth. The hovering inspectors wouldn't get it. His audience seemed to have the sense of humor of a hunk of metal, which he felt was ironic, all things considered.

The female inspector yanked his head to the side and jabbed an implement in his ear. It felt like a toothpick, but it looked like a nightmare.

"This is incredibly fucking uncomfortable."

Her gaze fell on him like he was nothing more than Polly's potted plant. He had never been treated this coldly. Alex remembered being loved, as he remembered feelings, scents, colors, places, and people.

He was starting to suspect memories were faulty things, however.

He couldn't be sure of how static his life had been. Perhaps some of it was, but the broken images were proof enough that what he had known had pieces missing. Pieces missing that seemed filled in by things he was endeared to, a color-by-numbers approach.

A painted life, inked in lines, connected with color.

"Al. Alex. Hey. Are you ok?"

"Yeah, Percy. I'm fine. Just thinking about..." She didn't correct him.

He remembered their names in fleeting loose-leaves, half-written and half transposed. At first, in little starts and stops, but now they came back as if drowning, especially when he dreamed.

Alex, a bright red creature of the black sea, would float on by and be deluged by words. Then, each syllable's taste, smell, and color would explode and boil the ocean around him.

The inspector made a noise while checking her tablet, leaving the toothpick from hell lodged firmly in his ear. He winced.

"You aren't supposed to respond like that."

"Alright, then let me shove a toothpick into your ear canal and see how you feel about it, you sadistic fuckface," he spat with a sneer. She merely blinked vacantly.

"Toothpick? Fuckface?"

Clearly, he was speaking a different language than she was.

Polly covered her mouth with her hand, hiding her large smile behind manicured nails. He could see her diaphragm moving behind her skin as she laughed to herself, silently.

"Are you going to make it?" Polly asked behind her hand.

"No." He gave her a grimace. She gave him an exaggerated frown. She was a giving-thing, it seemed. But a sensation, not unlike the toothpick from hell shoved in his ear, told him this might not be entirely true.

The female inspector wrenched his head back and started poking around in his mouth, jabbing an instrument into the back of his throat. Polly drew a sharp inhale as the instrument descended. At least he didn't need to breathe to live.

In fact, he had no gag reflex whatsoever.

Alex wanted to make an inappropriate joke. He seemed filled with them and compelled to blurt them out whenever possible.

However, as he opened his mouth to speak, the stern male inspector snapped a glove over his hand in a genuine threat.

Al wouldn't be making his joke. Instead, the man pressed his chest, a piece of plasticine clicked open, and this action struck the robot mute.

Alex looked down at his insides, blue and buzzing with chemicals, but with all the trappings of normal organs. He had a heart of sorts, a painfully bright, powerful core that sat within his chest a bit to the left of center. It blinded even him to look at for too long.

"This is going to be uncomfortable."

"Uh-huh."

The male inspector pushed his fingers in between Alex's 'heart' and 'rib cage' and tugged at something. Alex instantly shot Polly—who was staring at the ministrations behind her hands—a look of white-hot terror. She quickly covered her eyes, and yet she still watched between the gaps. If only to offer him comfort.

"Can you…stop molesting my inner organs, please and thank you?"

"I'm finished."

The inspector took his gloves off and tossed them into a trash receptacle, a bit of blue fluid lingering over the rim.

"It seems to be in working order, but its responses as you intimated are out of scope. I am unsure if—"

"Thank you, Stefan. It's important he's adjusting accordingly; however, I think he's important to study—"

Stefan raised his hand to cut her words in half.

"I'm going to stop you there, Andra. You've done an adequate job, but it's not your project."

Stefan leaned forward to the curve of Polly's ear and whispered, low in his throat.

"You are too close to this, An. Make sure it behaves as expected. Others may not be as kind to its responses as Poppy or I have."

Poppy began to unhook the very lifelike, very pissed off robot. Stefan turned to help her, and soon they were finished manhandling him, leaving Alex sitting stark naked.

"Can you get me some fucking pants? What is it with you people and stripping me?" Alex glared at Stefan and Poppy beneath his strong brows.

"...very good," Stefan said nothing-words, shooting Polly a warning glance. Alex's expression turned to poison.

The pair left and the glass door shut behind them with a hiss and a click.

"Polly."

"Yes, right, sorry!" Polly scrambled to attention and clicked over on her gold heels to pick up his plain clothes. Alex took the pants from her and pulled them on without a scrap of decency.

She looked away, giving him the modesty he was not bothering to give her.

"You don't have to look away," he said, still poisonous.

"...why wouldn't I...?"

"I'm not human, remember? I'm an 'it'. An 'it' you want to study, right? I'm a science project."

Polly stood with his shirt clenched in her hand as he snapped and velcroed his pants.

"So you heard..."

"Of course I heard. I have incredible hearing. Speaking of which, the pharmacist who makes your 'anti-emo pills' just a few rooms down really hates his job and wishes his wife was dead," he said, hand on his hip, staring out beyond the walls at the sounds of people.

"I guess the complaints are the same, even centuries later." Alex snatched his shirt out of Polly's hands and pulled it over his head.

"I want to get some work done," he blurted out beneath the fabric.

"...excuse me?"

"I don't look like myself. And I want my tattoos back," Alex muttered as the shirt came over his head.

"That's ridiculous...tattoos are outlawed."

"Yeah, yeah, I know. Outlawed for anyone below some arbitrary classist ceiling. So is sex, drugs, rock and roll, and fun. Never fun. No more fun, ever."

Polly hugged herself and swiveled her ankle. She seemed to have a habit of trying to make herself smaller when wounded.

"...I don't even know what...what would work on you.."

"You're a cosmetics engineer, aren't you?" he asked, looking over her conflicted stance.

"Yeah, but they don't teach us outlawed practices..." Polly replied, raising a palm to emphasize her point.

Alex ducked to look into one of the monitors and ruffled

his hair. Then came putting on his shoes, not that he needed to wear them anyways.

"Besides, The Director doesn't want me changing your face."

"Fuck the Director," he hissed, a viper coiled in a shell.

"Alex, you can't just go around saying things like that."

"I won't. When I'm here, I'm me. When I'm out there, I'm 'it'. I get it, Polly, really I do." Al walked towards the worrying girl and placed his strong hands on her sloped shoulders.

"…no one up here will do that for you," she said in willowed words.

"…ok. So, where would we go?"

"We'd have to go Below," Polly said, avoiding his gaze.

"Which is where, exactly?" Alex insisted, hands still yet on her shoulders.

"It's where they keep…discouraging people."

Alex removed his hands from her shoulders and placed a hand on his hip.

"It's a ghetto?" he mused behind a sneer, "not much has changed, after all."

"…yes. That's a word from your time, but yes."

"Would they get in trouble for fixing me up?" he asked, his bright blue gaze piercing right through her.

"No, but you probably will. You're tracked. You're going to need to clear us to go down there…I don't have that kind of clearance."

Polly held up her wrist and showed him a pale blue design.

"It's a barcode," he reasoned, disquieted that they were both things to catalog, track, and measure.

"Yup. Didn't you notice you had one?"

"…no. I just assumed it was a tattoo," Alex replied, bluntly. Polly snorted, exasperated with the robot who quite simply didn't want to admit he was one.

"You aren't who you were before."

"….I know."

"And when I said study, I didn't mean like a lab rat. I meant…like something we've never seen before. Like a real person…" Polly flicked his chest with her finger making a dull thunk, "…beneath all that stupid plastic, or whatever."

"Well, fuck you very much," he said with a half-smile.

Polly's mouth drew up into a smirk as she took Al's wrist and held up the barcode.

"You can go anywhere you want, but they'll know. Now that you've been cleared."

"We," he corrected her.

"Huh?" she replied, holding his wrist inertly.

"We can go anywhere we want."

Alex took Polly by the shoulder, his strong arms wrapping around her protectively, and approached the door. She dug in her gold spokes as they moved. He noticed.

The door opened for them with a slight hiss, and when they stepped on through, a pleasant click followed.

Alex looked down the hallway to the left and then the right. The air felt dead, like nothing living had ever drawn breath within these hallways. The adjacent rooms, so small and lined like closets, were far louder with the sounds of people. Yet, he had to focus to hear the words beyond.

"It's so...quiet."

He heard no laughter. It sounded nothing like the streets he remembered. No screaming, no cars, no sirens, no children. He smelled no cigars, nor greasy Chinese food, no pizza, no coffee, nothing. He felt no snow, he saw no sun, and he didn't like any of it.

And there were no cigarettes.

"...pull up the partition," Polly warned the robot wonder.

"...fine, Mom."

He fell back into himself like a stone, his consciousness taking the reins loosely as the other operating system acted as his steed. He fancied himself as an administrator, though how accurate a label, he couldn't say.

They approached the elevator as he held up his wrist and swiped it before the opening. They stepped inside, and Polly took his arm from her shoulder. The arm laid lifeless by his side, and she keened her head to look into his eyes.

"Are…you still in there?" she whispered.

"Hello, Second. Which floor do you require?" A caustically pleasant synthetic female voice chimed around them.

"P15." The knowledge was within him; he had but to whisk his mental fingertips and let it float beyond his lips.

"Of course. Please proceed with caution and remember that You Are Loved, You Are Valued, and You Are Special."

The elevator moved slowly at first, and then altogether quickly, the gravity kicking in, so the two were inert. They bolted through space, down, down, to the depths of hell.

Polly searched his face. He seemed to be ignoring her or quite simply wasn't processing stimuli. But when the elevator finally stopped, and she stepped through, he caught her hand in his own.

"Can I switch now?"

"We've got to pass a gate first. After," Polly said, hushing him with a gentle gesture.

Al nodded and stepped after her, letting his hand drop away. It was dark. What was once sterile and white became brown-smelling and foul.

As they walked, stark white lights gave way to blue and red ones. Familiar color, and the unmistakable scent of garbage, marked the line between civilization and everything else.

"Sir."

The guard before them was dressed in black with an obnoxious looking laser rifle. Alex thought the guards wore white but hadn't seen one yet, and quickly engaged the partition to find out why. He guessed if you were stationed down here, you didn't get one of the fancy white getups with the slick chrome weapons. The geometry in his vision told him this in yellow shapes and sprawling text.

"What are you here for…and what about the girl?"

The man gave Alex a sly look and moved his hand over his slick mouth. Alex knew that look yet kept himself from sneering. He was pulling on his reins too tightly.

"Business or pleasure?"

"Pleasure," the obvious answer between the two options; he had known men like this. They existed in every time and every place. They were easy to dispose of once you knew which trick worked best on which target.

"Nice."

Alex held back the explosive urge to ditch the partition and strangle the life from this one. It'd be so terribly easy, and he surprisingly relished the idea. Instead, he took the guard's glossy name-tag between his fingers and scanned his file from his name and number.

"Brahms. George Brahms?"

"Y-yeah. Yes, sir."

"Very good, Brahms. You're due for a promotion, aren't you?"

"Yes, sir!" Another guard walked towards them with a dumb grin painted on his face. He had his gun slung over his shoulder and stood with his hand on his hip. They seemed like caricatures of guards, written poorly.

"Howdy, sir." Alex disregarded this one on the grounds that 'howdy' was a stupid phrase.

"I will push the process along," Alex said, mechanically.

"Great!"

"Man, you're going to get a better pass and everything... get to have your fun without the Judge batting a damned eye."

Alex quietly filed a motion to Hard Reset Brahms and walked on by, taking Polly by the elbow, who jerked forward on her golden heels. She played the part of a resisting damsel a bit too convincingly.

"Gentleman." Both guards stood at attention and saluted —a caricature. "S-sir!"

He rolled his eyes once out of their line of vision and dragged his companion like a heavy sack.

"Y-you didn't really...promote him, did you?" Polly asked, ducking to his ear as she feigned stumbling.

"Nope."

"Then what?" she asked, tilting her head to try to catch Alex's gaze.

"He's going to be sent out an airlock in three days," he said with a vicious half-smirk.

Polly dug her heels to halt them both, scouring his face with her deep brown eyes. He finally pulled down the protocols in full. Baby blues came back to life while the liquid of his irises swirled with thousands upon thousands of lines of code.

"Are...you serious?"

"Deadly fucking serious," Alex retorted with a Cheshire grin on his face, "Good thing you vouched for me, huh? Better to have me in this tin can than...whoever I used to be..."

"…yeah. Remind me not to piss you off, or whatever."

"Reminder Set: Two weeks from now: morning wake cycle. Andra Polly Verdane at the ass crack of dawn.."

"You…didn't really set a reminder, did you?"

"No," Alex replied, with a mischievous glimmer in his eye, paired with a devious quirk of the lip.

Polly hadn't noticed these little tells and instead took to walking ahead of him, arms crossed.

When confronted with what civilization lived here, Alex stood speechless, while Polly trudged onwards. The gutter flowers of children with dirty faces and hungry gazes took root in the shadowed brush. Hundreds, if not thousands, of people were speaking, bartering, struggling, and suffering.

The smells of New York were a familiar, distant memory; the ripeness of summers spent in untidy boroughs prickled the back of his mind.

This space was a caricature of the time before. Transposed and mangled to its most basic, most harrowing elements.

"Where are they getting the cabbage from?" Alex asked, gesturing to a fresh food stand stocked solely with cabbages. Nothing else in this place appeared fresh, real, and ripe. Long-expired food lined various stalls; things that would keep longer, preserved, pickled, yet mostly putrid.

These plants were green and inviting.

"The black market. It's run by one of the Section Firsts, or so I hear…I don't really know."

"You don't know?" Alex asked, tilting his head as he glimmered over the healthy green colors in his wake.

"Hey, I'm not even supposed to, like, know that much…" Polly stammered out. She wrapped her arms around herself and looked at the people as they flooded around the pair. She scraped her hair behind her ear after she spoke.

"You've…never been here before," he reasoned.

"Hey! Spare some creds?" A small boy with bright eyes outstretched his wrist, and Alex noticed the tell-tale blue design on his wrist.

"Are they supposed to have the—"

"They aren't…supposed to…I don't—"

Alex paused for a second and swiped his wrist over the boy's without a second thought. The boy's eyes widened instantly.

"Woah…a hundred?" he gasped, then raised his wrist to the sky, "Hey! This guy's just givin' out hundreds!"

A crowd began to form around Polly and Alex, as what had once been the ebb and flow of suffering was now a sea of need. They were battered immediately.

"Alex!" Polly yelped, jostled between what seemed like hundreds of hungry hands.

"Let's get out of here," he huffed, snagging her wrist from between the ocean of people and jerking her after him.

Alex was faster than he was used to, and Polly began to lag behind. It took a moment for him to notice he'd lost her, but when he did, he turned back to sweep her into his arms.

He immediately popped up with one foot over an oil drum, launching over a perforated wall.

She screamed the entire way down, colors and air whipping around her as they plummeted. Not skipping a beat, Alex placed her on her feet as she wobbled on shaking legs.

"…are you crazy?! Oh my god!!" she gasped out, struggling as the adrenaline surged down to her very fingertips.

"No. I'm a fucking robot ninja," he said with a satisfied smirk.

"Is everything a joke to you?" she asked, still visibly shaken. She dusted off her clothes and turned around to look at her rear.

"My…ass is dirty. Already."

"Your ass is alive at least…I think we lost them." The blonde pitched his exceptional hearing, but the crowd must have dispersed like dye in water. He heard nothing but the usual sounds of a bustling market.

"Yeah…I mean, you probably shouldn't give credits out so freely," she admitted, still trying to dust herself off. Somehow she had dirt in her mouth. Polly spit but found no purchase.

"What? Why?" Alex spat, hand finding itself on his hip as it had in the laboratory/prison.

"Didn't you have poor people in your time period?"

"…yeah and…I…bought them sandwiches," Alex replied, confidence waning.

"Should've bought him a sandwich, then," she said with a knowing tilt of the brow.

Alex snorted and took Polly's hand in his own. He felt her heart beating through her warming skin. He felt so much colder than she was.

"…are you okay?" he asked.

"Y-yeah, I'm…why do you ask?"

"Your heart is still racing."

He felt the pulse through her fingers. He heard it in his ears. He loved that heart, that pulse, that blood, the bones, the muscles. Everything about her, he loved, because she was Percy. Even that strange clicking sound her jaw made now and then was loved by him.

Polly squeezed his hand back yet said nothing. He squinted as he looked at her, the geometry that read out her vitals buffering until he stopped trying to burn her after-image into his eyes.

"We need to find a mechanic and a cosmetics engineer..." she trailed as he studied her.

"Know where to start looking?" he asked.

"...nope," she said with a distant expression on her face.

"...God damn it, Polly."

"Hey! Hey, don't get mad at me..."

The two bickered as they walked. Like he had bickered with Percy. Snide comments, friendly flirting, and pleasant drama. Time had changed nothing, he thought.

Alex stared at her as she talked and traced her face with his eyes, catching the tiny blonde facial hair that she tried to hide, yet everyone living had. He remembered her magenta mouth, so very pale now, and the bright-colored clothes she once wore. She had been a fan of fashion, and now, it had all been bleached away.

"You look just like her."

"But...I'm not her." Polly dipped below a tarp that painted her in cornflower blue.

"Are you so sure?" He stepped under that same tarp, the color of his eyes competing for dominance.

"What do you mean?" She searched his face for an easy answer. Her lip quirked like a machine's hitch when she couldn't find it.

"...do you ever wonder about time?" he asked an innocuous sentence, one that made Polly worry her pale lips.

Alex picked up a piece of raw metal from the cobbled floor and began to bend it into shape. He easily twisted it around with his fingers, making a flower: simple lines, nothing fancy, just a daisy.

"...no?"

Alex played with the metal flower, pulling at the makeshift petals to form them into something more deliberate. A symbol of a flower, but still recognizable.

"…of all the people that would have been alive now, you're here, and you look just like her. Of all the people who would've taken care of me and made sure I 'acclimated'…."

"They picked me," Polly blurted out, wrapping her arms around herself to appear smaller.

"Yes, but you don't realize how much you look like her, do you?" The blue of his eyes was a black hole for the cosmetician. It was hard for Polly to look away.

She touched her face as they talked and looked away from him, her worried gaze grazing the cobbled steps before her feet.

"Of all the people with all the names that have ever been, your middle name is Polly. It sounds like Percy."

"It's just a coincidence," she exclaimed.

They ducked underneath a yellow tarp, and Alex stopped her. Her face was painted in the color of sunrise, golden wheat, and umber earth.

"Are you sure?"

"…n—"

"What's your favorite color?" Before Polly could answer, he told her.

"Pink. Bright magenta pink, and you like green as well. But I'm guessing they don't let you wear that here."

"How…" his words barreled over her own.

"You're self-conscious because of some scar you have, and you almost never wear anything short. You are going to want to tell me it was an accident, and I'm going to tell you that you did it to yourself. And I'm going to be right."

Polly glared as he drew her feelings from the back of her

skull. Stars of light flickered at the corner of her eyes. Stars of light that should be dead considering the 'anti-emo pills' flooding in her system.

"And let me guess…you started off as a secretary," he said, raising his finger to punctuate his point.

"You read my files. It proves nothing except that you don't mind your own business—"

"I read none of it. And they'd never include 'self-harm' on the record of a perfectly spotless cosmetics tech who looks exactly like my old best friend."

"It doesn't mean anything…"

"Sure, Polly. Keep telling yourself that."

Alex patted his pockets and remembered he didn't have cigarettes, considering they weren't supposed to be made anymore, and if they were, they were contraband.

Silence cut into their time together, with Polly no longer holding his hand, and Alex with his jaw clenched. They walked on, the two casting purple shadows as lights beside them ebbed and flowed in dim yellow circles.

"..what were you looking for?" she asked.

"Something to wrap my lips around," Polly snorted at his response.

"Seriously? Like…what?"

"Don't look at me like that—a cigarette, what else?"

"They're contraband."

"I know."

"And it wouldn't do anything for you anyways…"

Alex stuck the metal flower in his pocket and pressed on. They didn't know what they were looking for. They didn't know who they were looking for. They didn't know if they'd have another encounter like the mob of hungry hands from earlier.

A girl with a flower on her shirt and curls of blonde hair darted past their shared orbit. She had a constellation of freckles, with sharp, almond-shaped eyes set above her cheeks.

He stopped, standing perfectly still on limbs that wanted nothing more than to break beneath him. If he had air in his lungs, it would've been sucked clean out. His heart would've dropped to the floor in an instant. She was an apparition.

"Olive."

The girl scrunched her face up and waved her wrist at a merchant. She was complaining loudly.

"…Olive? Oh, right…no. I mean…she's not, obviously."

"….yes. Yes, she is."

"Are you sure you're functioning?" Polly shot back.

"I'm positive," he said, voice a whisper against the gravity of the small woman before them.

The little thing with her cat-like eyes, large ears, and short stature turned to look at the pair who had stopped to look at her. She was caught in a frozen still-frame, her eyes closing slowly as time ground to a halt.

She resumed her 'negotiating' with the merchant.

"阿呆!"

It took a few moments for him to remember how his face worked, but that phrase made Alex smile brighter than any star in the sky.

POLLY; there's so much to say for Polly, and yet she swallows her words even now. Yet soon, she won't.

Polly, prior to meeting the disruptive war-machine, wove through her days like any other blanched worker bee, but at night, she wrote.

She wrote while sitting at her desk in her room with a pencil she found in storage. They were poems on errant leaves of paper she had claimed.

Most people didn't know how to handle poetry anymore, let alone writing that wasn't technical documentation. Even the elite only had a passing fascination with emotions they'd never have to feel; the best art comes from strong emotions and empathizing therein, and hers were visceral, to say the least.

Polly had written several phrases of feelings this morning before Alex was inspected. She hadn't had time to hide her painful little papers. And now, as both Alex and herself were in the bowels of their planet-sized ship, meandering after a vague idea, to get some illegal work done, for a very vain robot, she had forgotten she'd left them in her pocket.

As if on cue, he dug his hand into her pocket to place the metal daisy he'd made there, but he stilled. Alex pulled out a small note and held it between his fingers as Polly jumped at him in protest.

"No! Oh my god—give it back, you shithead!" Alex stepped back to avoid her painted claws.

"Ah, you're so mad…what is this, a love letter? To me?" Alex swung around as she scrambled to latch to his arm.

Alex held his hand up above her head to taunt her.

"Please! Don't!" She clamored and dug her nails into his skin. It hurt, but not enough to make him stop. It was the memory of pain.

"…why are you so upset? It just looks like some bad poetry…" he paused, turning the paper in his hand, "really…really bad 'sad girl' poetry."

Polly looked to the dirty floor like a battered animal. The dirty floor looked back at her. She hated that floor. She hated, more than anything, that she felt the way she did when she knew she shouldn't, and feeling everything all the time made it hard to live the life she had.

Her 'anti-emo pills,' as Alex had called them, had never worked, to begin with.

"…please. Alex."

"What? Everyone gets sad sometimes and writes really, really bad poetry. It's normal."

Alex held out the note in front of her face. A face that was not meant to explode with emotions. A face that was not meant to tremble and tremor so, as it was now, in a flash of something long since buried out of necessity.

Abruptly, Polly ripped the note away from him and prepared to shred it with her claws. Al raised a brow and studied her. He had seen Percy like this as well. They were not so different. In fact, they were exactly the same. Which meant he knew just what to say; it came on like breathing, this phrase.

"…you're allowed to feel, Polly." His words were like a bullet from a loaded gun.

He had used this phrase before, so very long ago, he remembered now.

He had used it when Percy had gotten off of her mind-numbing day job and found herself on his doorstep. He remembered her coming through his door, weaving around his disgusting mess, then planting her face, then her whole body, into his sofa.

Then, she'd groan for what felt like hours. He would say those words, and she'd tell him the story of her day.

"It's illegal!" Polly snapped, cutting Alex's trip down memory lane in two.

"To write or to feel? That's dumb. Also, look where we are," he snorted, "You think anyone here gives a shit?" the synth gestured around them. The colors might have been lively, but the people certainly weren't. They were barely hanging on and desperate for something more.

Alex wrapped an arm around her shoulder, and she flinched momentarily, the note crumpling tightly into her fist. She tried to make herself small, but he wasn't having any of that and curled his hand around her arm to keep her close.

Polly said nothing.

She said nothing as they waited for 'Not Olive'. She said nothing as Alex pushed her hair behind her ear. He fixed her coat while she said nothing and rubbed a bit of dirt from her face with his thumb. She was left naked in her speech-lessness.

With her chin in his hand, he stared at her until her large brown eyes focused on him.

"Tell me your poems. I'll always listen. And keep them forever," Alex said and tapped his temple with his pointer finger, "I'll remember every word. I'm a computer, aren't I?"

Polly said nothing, yet she felt…everything.

MAYA HAD BEEN INVESTIGATING other ways to get what she wanted. Maya was no different than Polly in her desire for something richer. Be that emotions, or quality of life.

However, sometimes human desires outpace reach. Sometimes goals break apart with the strain. Sometimes, no matter how hard you try, you can't make things work or make them better. That didn't mean, however, that she wouldn't try.

The barkeep didn't have what she needed. 'Olive' popped out of the 'dive bar'—as Alex called it—with a sour expression.

Had Maya the unlimited resources, she would have had a much different life. She worked hard for brilliance. Alex had simply been given it and could download anything he wanted to know in mere seconds and surpass her without any required effort.

They were completely different.

Alex tapped Polly on the shoulder, who turned to see 'Not Olive,' shoving her hands into her pockets to find something, but only pulling out some crumbs and lint. They stood beneath an enclave of sunrise-orange, watching her.

"You're...sure she can help us, or whatever?" Polly asked, staring at the back of his blond head. Her gaze lingered on the indented ports in his neck.

"Yes. I'm positive," he said softly.

"How can you be so sure?"

Alex took her hand and held it between his cold fingers, then laced those fingers between her own. Polly felt awkward but took to a familiar stride.

"Because I'm sure."

With a quick movement, Alex reached out to grab the small girl as she wiped her hands on her pants. That token 'Olive' snarl flared up, as he knew it would.

"Hey! What gives, buddy? I ain't got nothin' for you..." the little machinist spat.

"I heard you were looking for a power cell. Or several. And before you ask, I have excellent hearing."

Alex kept Polly's hand in his own. She had stepped behind him to hide, eyeing the shorter woman beyond the treeline of his shoulder.

"Yeah...what's it to ya'?" The small thing had managed to rid the grime and put her hands on her hips. Her mouth was stuck in a petulant, woodland-critter grimace.

"I've got one. Or several. And I need your help. Do you know if there's anyone around who can do work on me? Purely cosmetic."

Maya began to circle the duo with her hands still on her hips, her chest puffed out.

"Mm...I...can do it fer you," she hummed.

Alex turned back to Polly with a look that burned

brighter than the stars. Her brows raised significantly at both his expression and the machinist's answer.

"It's...this isn't happening," Polly muttered to herself, slinking back further behind Alex's shoulder.

"Yeah? Great. Lead the way, princess," Al said with a quirked grin. Maya's nose scrunched up as she waved at the two to follow her. Polly trailed behind Alex, who walked tall and strong. She, less so, but she grew confident with each step.

Shadows from the dull lamps above filtered over their faces. They passed by brown-smelling stalls. Alex stopped at a man slumped over, his addled head tilted on its axis, staring at nothing and everything.

"What's wrong with him?"

"What, ya' never seen a guy dipped outta' his gourd?" Maya said with a slight turn of her head. They ascended small grated steps, despite Alex reeling back as if compelled.

"...dipped?"

"Drugged," their little leader replied.

Polly's face blossomed into a mixture of what can only be described as disbelief and disgust.

"That's...not possible. Drugs are illegal without a—."

"Well, they ain't here. They give 'em to us cause they know our lives are crap."

"So it's a proper ghetto then," Alex said with a sneer.

They stopped at a plateau of grates, and Polly took her hand back, to frown and scowl. Disbelief was a creature comfort, and she kept it close to the chest.

"...Ya got names?"

"Alex. I'm a—"

"Yeah, a synth. A particularly shitty one at that. Don't

think I dunno' who you are. Yer different than last time…not shittin' up the brothels or—"

Alex cracked a smile and chuckled, out of turn.

"I'm Polly…what are you laughing about?"

"Guess my prior version wasn't so blank, after all," this amused him, "She's brash as all hell, isn't she?" he added.

"She has a name, ya' know…Maya." The short woman extended her hand, and Alex shook it in a firm grasp. Polly did the same and resumed her perpetual state of distress.

"Smart name for a smart girl." Maya glared as Alex spoke.

"You even talk different…last time ya' walked through me. Called me a roach.."

"Did I? Damn, I'm an asshole," he mused on this, hand stroking his chin deviously.

"…you're weird."

"He is, isn't he?" Polly agreed.

"Well, come inside. I ain't got all day, ya know."

Maya opened a small door, and both Alex and Polly had to duck to clear the frame. The roof was low, and the innards were damp, dark, and joyless.

Maya smashed her closed fist onto a button on the wall, and the small hovel lit up with hundreds of LED lights. A glimmer, a sparkle; color fashioned to make it bright and make it sing. They were Christmas lights, a remnant of the past.

As was Alex.

Maya sat herself down as Alex sat across from her at a table. Polly crouched at the far wall and tried to sit without her skirt riding up but wasn't successful.

"Don't be modest. We're in a ghetto trying to get some

black market plastic-fucking-surgery. The last thing you should be worried about is flashing people."

"Shut up, you big bucket of bolts..." Polly tugged at her skirt, wrenching at the fabric to conceal her thigh.

"Shouldn't have worn a skirt then, eh?" he teased.

"Shouldn't have worn your...stupid face!" she spat with a conflicted smile.

"Nice comeback, Poll. Anyways, I have...a picture of what I need."

Maya hefted a large toolbox onto the table, the shoddy thing whining under the weight.

"No problemo, pal. But first, the cell."

Alex grabbed the hem of his now perfectly dirty—once perfectly white shirt—and pulled it over his head.

"What are you doin'?"

"Hush."

With the shirt gone, he pressed his hand to his chest, and with a slight click came the disgusting display of synthetic internal organs. Polly visibly blanched.

"You aren't going to..."

"Yup," he replied.

"Wicked..." Maya's mouth was agape. She reached for the core, but Alex shut his chest before her tiny, sticky little fingers got a chance to meddle with his insides.

"After. First, you fix my face. And give me tattoos."

"...that's...all you want?" she asked, thin brow raising.

"Yeah. That's all I want."

Polly crossed her arms, happy she didn't have to see Maya plug around inside his guts. Her golden heels scraped at the grates on the floor as she propped herself up as comfortably as she could.

"…nice poster," Alex said, eying the half-mechanical woman painted on a piece of preserved paper.

Maya had been fiddling with her tools, screwing thin metal into plugs and ports, and hand-cranking a strange device. Her attention was stolen with that one phrase.

"Thanks!"

"That's the Major, right? I saw it in '95…I think? I might have been…'busy' at the time…hold on. Might as well show you…"

Maya was dumbfounded. Even more so when Alex tapped at his temple and pulled out a long, thin wire from the back of his neck. With nimble fingers, he plugged it into a port on the wall. A small, decrepit looking projection sputtered to life parallel Polly.

The image flickered in a storm of black and white static. Finally, a moving picture fluttered before them, cut off by a neat row of chairs that dipped every now and then.

"I don't remember this playing in theaters…" he said, squinting at the projection.

"That's…her name? Major?" Maya's eyes were as big as saucers. She scrambled over to sit closer, very clearly blocking the display with much of her head.

"I don't remember. I'm guessing that bit of information got lost in time."

"I…didn't know you had moving pictures," Polly said, trying to push Maya out of the way who fought her for the best view. They were like children.

"I have a lot of them. But only the parts I remember… turns out I have a shitty memory."

"Or I just liked to get laid at the cinema," he offered with naked honesty.

Alex crossed his arms and let the two girls watch. To

Maya, this meant something far different than Polly's awe at the spectacle.

In all her animated glory, this powerful woman who was flipping about the screen spoke a language she knew bits and pieces of—the subtitles filled in the rest.

"That's all I got." The screen died, and Alex pulled up a series of stills of himself, having looked into mirrors for most of his life.

"…Major," Maya said.

"I don't remember, sorry."

"Why was she naked?" Polly asked, squinting in the low light.

"It's so she can turn invisible. It has something to do with her suit. Right? Yeah. I may even have that capacity. I'm not sure yet."

Maya didn't say a word and went back to fiddling with her tools.

"…you okay, Maya?" asked the blond synth. His eyes were warm as he looked at the plucky apparition. She avoided the sunlight of his gaze.

"Yeah…I've just never seen somethin' like this…what did ya mean by '95?"

"He's old."

"Like…3095?"

"Back more," Alex said as he flipped through the images to one of his face, fingers flexing in the air. He sought the clearest frame, which was a feat considering how crippled every image was.

"…2095?"

"Back."

"No way," Maya gasped out in disbelief.

"Back."

"1995?"

"Well, my last memories end in 1997. I'm not sure why. But yes, 1995," he paused for a moment, "that's the back-story, anyway." Alex's eyes flickered back and forth, searching for where that sentence lived.

Maya started to laugh and ended her giggles with a snort fit for a queen.

"Queen of pigs, as always," the blond chuckled.

"That's a load of shit," the little machinist spat.

"No, it isn't. I formatted him," Polly said, moving to sit in her spot, her back to the wall.

"…wild…"

"Sounds just like something she'd say—"

"Wait! Who's that?! Stop! Stop the stupid reel thingy!" Maya punctuated her sentence by pointing.

Alex went back a few files by flexing his fingers. He stopped at a still frame of Olivia and Percy sharing ice cream as snow fell around them. The pair were laughing about something. The next few frames were scattered. It took a moment, but he managed to salvage some sound and video.

"You're, like, such a nightmare, Liv. It's, like, freezing out or whatever!"

"Why? I just wanted some sweets. You don't have ta' be such a b—"

The video cut out, the rest of the noise scraping with mechanical clutter. The frames shattered, colors mangled, and the video ended with Alex's hand in the shot.

"…that girl.."

"Olive," he said softly.

Maya shoved her goggles on her face and fired up one of her machines. It made a terrible noise and vibrated her entire arm.

"Face first," he insisted.

"Naw. I want you to tell me 'bout the girl with the pink. And the other one, that looks like her. So we're doin' the tattoos first..."

"I didn't realize how much we look like them, or whatev—" Polly placed her hand to her mouth to stop the words. Her eyes shot up to look at Alex. He had a smile on his face. Al flipped to the clearest image of his tattoos he could find.

"I'm lucky," he said with a broad smile.

"How do ya' figure?" Maya asked with a disgruntled look on her face.

"I found you both."

"...I'm not sure if you're just crazy or we're all—"

"Tell me 'bout the pink girl," Maya interrupted Polly mid-sentence, not looking at either of them.

Alex breathed in deeply as Maya punctured his skin with the device, eyeing his pictures as she worked. He didn't flinch, but he did feel the pain clearly now. It was comforting. Pain meant you were alive.

He exhaled. Inhaled. Exhaled. Then, he told her everything.

ALEX WAS SPLAYED flat and pinned like an insect. Maya's sharp instruments were perched with levers and pulleys far too close to parts he'd rather not lose. Wincing, he screwed his eyes shut. She began the laborious work of etching his skin in inked stories, each quite detailed and full of symbols.

With brows knit, the small girl stooped over him, partially climbing, partially hovering. She had her tongue sticking out of the corner of her mouth as she worked.

Polly had fallen asleep with her head propped up on her hand. Her elbow rested on a dirty box, covered in grime, and her legs were curled at her chest. Alex remembered that snore. She could give a chainsaw a run for its money.

As she had work and had slept through her shift, she was bound to face the consequences. Consequences that would never reach her, however, because her confidant was who he was. And so, he let her sleep soundly.

Alex got a knee to the groin, shaking him from his thoughts, which wouldn't have been a problem a few days ago. The pain was dull at first. The remembrance of pain, and nothing more. Then, it felt like he was being shot up into his ribs through his dick.

His eyes burst open as he glared at Maya, but she wasn't paying attention. Instead, she focused on the lines, each more complex than the next. The colors were bright, then dark, then the color of blood. Maya noticed the story the pictures told; it was hard not to.

"Yer like a picture-book, heh," the little machinist said, still yet focused on her work and not at all registering Alex's boiling glare.

Pink faced, her light curls swiped his chest as her head bowed, and she worked on detailing the poppies that bloomed on the bones of his hips. The needle vibrated through his plasticine skin, a comforting agony, far more comforting than her bony little elbow.

Al raised his head and stared beneath thick, manicured brows. He didn't like looking like a ponce straight out of a magazine spread. But what he liked even less was the small machinist's attempt at busting his junk with her fucking bones.

"Elbow," he grunted.

"Huh?"

"Are you trying to neuter me?" he hissed behind clenched teeth.

Maya sat up and wiped her slick forehead with her forearm. She maintained her weight on his groin to steady herself. Confusion swept her face as she stared down at him, her cat-like eyes narrowing.

The drill-bit monstrosity within her hand whirled. She turned and tapped it into a small tray of ink. Many other small trays were lined up near her of varying colors. It was a menagerie of pigment; flowers bled out in small dishes. She seemed a master even at color, of all things.

"…but you don't.."

"I do." He needed her to believe him. He needed her to stop trying to puncture his family jewels with her bony little body.

"Bull fucking shit…" she said with a sneer, turning back to continue her precise work, "Let me see," she added a bit too enthusiastically.

"Fuck no! Hurry your ass up, princess, I have shit to do."

The machinist made a disgruntled whine and switched positions. She also might have purposefully jabbed her elbow into his groin again.

Olivia would have done the same.

Polly shifted slightly and began to rock her head forward with tiny stops and starts. She was slipping from her own grasp and caught herself as the weight of her skull threatened to smack her head into her knees. Polly made an incredibly loud snort, which startled Maya. The inevitable came to pass.

"What the fuck!?" the blond synth bellowed as the needle scraped up across his flesh in a jagged, angry line.

Polly hadn't fully stirred, and as he seethed behind his bared fangs, the cosmetician asked a simple question, her mouth full of sleep.

"Mm…what time is it?" Blonde hair matted and a mess from the cruel, foul heat of the under-dwelling, Polly pulled it back behind her ears and yawned, smacking her lips.

She suffered to swipe through her internal digital display to find the answer to her question. A dream had claimed her and was refusing to let her search properly. Her eyes were still so full of sleep and sun and more.

She had dreamed of a real sun over a watercolor sky. She had dreamt of drinking what must have been alcohol but didn't know how she knew that. It was thin, yellowed, and sour. It made her feel dizzy and light.

She had dreamt about looking across a city of colors while she drank. The sky grew bright before her eyes.

A blond man with freckles around his nose met her gaze, and she felt the cold come in as the temperature dropped. Here, they had real seasons.

She saw the cityscape compete with the stars that fought to stay afloat above it. The sky was salmon pink until the sun rose above the thin line of the horizon. Purple gave way to orange around the glowing ball in the sky, until the light threatened to blind them both.

He told her something with a flutter of lips on her ear. Here in this dream, she was not afraid of this closeness. It filled her with light more than the strange drink did.

"He did something fucking stupid..." the blond man said, face obscured.

"Couldn't, like, compete with our weird-ass sexless marriage..." she replied.

She felt like he had done something but didn't know what. Something wrong and raw because he couldn't look at her. Or rather, she couldn't make out his face. She felt her mouth move to ask him something, but nothing came out.

She also felt something blossoming in her chest. A feeling. A sensation. Smart snippets of an idea, framed around someone with a small mouth, and a shock of pink hair, crept in. She didn't know this feeling, but looking at him, she felt it. It was so strong and so angry, and yet she was smiling.

At that moment, she saw the mark of some ancient figure

on his exposed shoulder where he had rolled his sleeves up, as the boy ran hot in any weather.

She remembered that...who was this? Where was she?

This was why sleep had clouded her. She wanted the drink and the cityscape. She wanted this sky, stars, sun, and light. She wanted to see his face. She wanted to know what that feeling had been.

Polly groggily perused her display for some semblance of time. Then, her focus was stolen, and gutted.

Her heart fluttered like a bird's wing against a bone cage. Her jaw clicked as her teeth ground down, and that heart hitched and kept on hitching.

Alex sat up. Polly stared behind dark brown lashes at his shoulder. A mark of some ancient figure stared back at her in angry black lines. It told her with its presence the answer she had been rebelling against. The answer she didn't want, from a question she hadn't ever been brave enough to ask; why could she feel so much?

"Just turn it into a river or something, fuck, I don't know..." he was speaking.

Alex was overcome with the fact that his entire side had been marred with a long jagged line. It looked like a river enough, with the nearby tattoos mimicking tall grass with their green lines.

"Then you'll power the food thingy up? Just to see if it works, yah?" Maya asked.

"Face first," he glared up at the little machinist.

"What's wrong with it? You look fine.." she said with a deep sigh.

Polly cleared her throat and spoke up.

"It isn't his..." she clarified, "...it isn't his face. That's why."

Maya rolled her eyes at the pair of them. Olivia would have done the same. And now, they both knew it.

Alex caught Polly staring at his shoulder tattoo. He smiled.

At that moment, an atmosphere control mechanic swiped his barcode at the main elevator.

Behind him, he left trees, birds, flowers, and insects. Before him, he was ascending into some new fresh hell of marble and white.

"Aw, come on ya' piece of shite…fack me…"

He bashed the control panel with rough hands, and finally, the machine began to move with his third, hardest smash.

He had a warm smile underneath his unruly flecks of sparse, wayward facial hair. On his head was a basic cap with a rim, green. Everything on his body was the same color. Uniform, but made of crumpled, cheap linen.

He had various tools at his belt, some plain and others fantastical.

The elevator stopped, and another ACM boarded from a different greenery tier. They had the same outfit and the same cap. The two twin trees stood side by side, planted firmly.

"Oye," the first ACM mumbled.

"Hey," the other man said with a rough grunt.

The second ACM played with a braided ring on his finger, then cleared his throat as the doors closed. They were moving to a floor marked with a bright star on the digital display, and the first ACM let out a whistle.

"Director mus' need it fixed bad if he's callin' The Greens, eh?" The first mechanic had a thick, unrefined accent.

"Usually gets a synthetic to fix it. I hate those fucking things..." The second one had an accent as well, but it was wholly different.

"Yah...what d'ya think changed, mate?"

The second ACM picked at his nails and grunted as he flicked dirt from beneath them onto the perfectly white floor of the elevator.

"I dunno. Maybe it's so important he can't trust a bucket o' bolts to do it for 'im."

"...why ya' hate somethin' that don't even piss or breathe proper, Larry? Ya' got such hatred in yer heart." The first ACM clenched his fist to his chest, then broke into a playful grin.

"I dunno, Henry, maybe because the minute that fu—fantastic leader of ours made some demon war-machine all this went to hell in a handbasket," Larry seethed out his words between his yellowed teeth.

"Yah...they started makin' more of 'em. Went on a rampage, roight? Some flung m'selves out'n air lock, yeh?" Henry offered, unsure of his words.

"You were about four when it started, Hen. I got years on you, and it wasn't always so utterly shit..." the other ACM continued.

"Ya, yer roight Larry."

The two men didn't talk for some time. As Henry looked around the elevator, he began to tap his hands on his sides. Then he started whistling, much to Larry's annoyance, so the other man took it upon himself to break the silence.

"Some say they get on, even if she's military. Not for me, no thank you, no sir…" Henry didn't respond.

Larry attempted to continue his rant, only to be stopped when the elevator jerked to a halt. They exited the elevator and stepped on slick, clean, white marble with swirls of pink and gold.

Henry and Larry were checked, patted down, and scanned. The guards were mercurial demons; they said nothing, and they didn't even sound like they were breathing. They looked like art pieces.

Henry looked up, but Larry kept his head down. Henry saw his reflection in one of their 'faces,' and he smartly looked away. Then Henry's eyes made a daring move, his head following.

He looked up to the ceiling. Those eyes drew ever wider, like a camera lens. He focused.

He breathed.

The ceiling above was painted with figures he only understood as concepts. Gods and goddesses, winged angels and horned demons in a cacophony on the arched ceiling of a room he could only give one word: godly.

The old gods fought on that spherical ceiling with clouds between their thighs. The clouds were dipped in pigments of plum and cerulean. The sky was smeared in bright blues, deep indigos, and yellowed on the horizon.

A man was nude on that ceiling, pointing to an older man as if he had been bestowed some immaterial greatness. At least that was what it felt like to Henry.

"Hen..." Larry tried to snap his friend out of his trance, but his rasped whisper fell on deaf ears.

"Henry...for God's sake..." It was a vestigial term. No one believed in God anymore.

Footsteps neared as the guards drew back and took formation. Henry didn't notice and took off his hat to hold in his rough hands. He was humbled by beauty he'd never seen before.

His eyes drew down, but the brows stayed up. He saw trees like the ones on his level but spindled with crystal–bright, sparkling, faceted into thousands of points of light.

He inhaled. The air smelled like flavors. Everything was alive and yet too beautiful to be real.

The footsteps stopped. Larry grabbed Henry's shoulder and tried to pull him down. Larry was kneeling. Henry shirked him off and continued to marvel.

A fountain made of solid marble grew out of the floor itself with gold-colored water catching the light. Bushes of strange fruits and odd gems dotted the room like they had grown organically from the rock.

A long table of black onyx set with many, many transparent stools. Within those stools were flowers, pressed between the panes of glass. The glass was spired and cut into fractals.

A synth was cutting a glistening gemstone out of a tree with a thin black blade. Her heels, seemingly a part of her feet, made her nearly as tall as the tree she was bending towards. She was nude, yet part of her was metal slick like the guards had been. She turned to round the tree, displaying a mass of wires draped like jewelry on the back of her skull.

"Do you like it?"

Larry swallowed hard and remained kneeling while Henry couldn't help but be overcome with emotion. His face grew more and more expressive with every passing moment. His heart felt like it would leap out of his chest. That he might die because this, this was something so beautiful, that he must have been on his way to someplace better.

A place called heaven, maybe.

"S'most beaut'ful thing I ever seen..." a prayer escaped his lips.

The man who spoke was the opposite of Henry's rough handsome awkwardness.

Henry was well-worn sandpaper on a piece of good cedar. Rugged, tan, and tall like the trees from The Greens.

This man was some kind of living statue. He didn't look a day over twenty-three, but looks were deceiving. Everything about him seemed polished to the point of being inhuman. He was tall. Quite a bit taller than the already tall Henry.

His attire was a dark suit inlaid with barely perceptible damask patterns.

Gray smoke escaped from the man's mouth, and that was when Henry realized he was smoking a cigarette.

"I though' art was...and that's...uh..." Henry's words fettered away with the smoke in the air.

"Forbidden? For you, yes," replied the new stranger.

"Oy...shite...you're..."

"Yes. Now stop gawking. You, stand. I am a busy man, and I need the sitting room perfect for tomorrow evening. And I need to verify the grand hall is just the perfect temperature. It's been terribly dry in both as of late and a bit too warm for my guests. The hall must be ready for next month."

"What's...goin' on tomorrow evenin'?" Henry dared to ask.

The Director perched the cigarette between his fingers, his pinky slightly extended until he folded his hand back to his mouth. The hand extended again in a choreographed dance.

He was as art, framed in dragon-spire smoke.

"A meeting. My ward returns to me."

Larry had finally stood and let his long arms dangle at his sides, daring for but a moment to look at the Director's face.

"An'...next month?" Henry asked, managing to look at the man for far longer than Larry had.

"A wedding," the Director said dryly, with a hint of disinterest, "Come."

The two men followed after the lord of their station. They walked on the floors he provided and breathed the sweet-smelling air he graciously gave them. Soon he'd have his judge, jury, and executioner at his side.

His "ward," so to speak.

However, he wouldn't be the same. He would be painted in trees, shapes, and old ideas. Letters from a language long since dead, a genre mark in eyes on his lower back, and poppies on his narrow hips. An angry symbol was now etched on that once perfect shoulder and a new river had been cut across his ribs from Maya's mistake.

His face and body would be his own.

The Director would not be happy about any of this.

Back down on the lower levels, Maya finished with the tattoos, and now came the matter of Al's face.

"I gotta turn you off.." Her words were blunt.

"What? Fuck no..."

"I really need to go. I'm going to get in so much trouble or whatever…" Polly stood awkwardly and fussed with her skirt. Turning slightly to dust off her rear, she saw a hideous smear. Her response to the gunk was a shrill shriek.

Maya and Alex winced in unison; she was loud enough to pierce glass.

"Poll, I'm second in command, right?"

"Yeah…" she said with the voice of a mouse.

"I say you can stay. I'll write you a hall pass or whatever the fuck they give you. I don't know."

Alex stared straight at Maya, who had her arms crossed, standing now at his side.

A machination whirled above him, and he would've blanched if he had red blood in his veins.

Maya picked up a print-out of a still from his memory and turned it over in her hands.

"I *have* ta' turn you off. It's delicate, and now that I know ya' can feel stuff, you'll feel it all if I don't. If ya' move, you could end up looking like that fat stain on Polly's fat ass..." Maya said with a piglet's snort.

"Hey!" Polly sneered and tried to wipe at it, but blackness and mucus came off on her hands.

"Totally gross. Like, what is this shit?" she grimaced.

"It's *some* kind of shit." Maya shrugged.

"That's not what I—oh…God..." Polly gagged in the back of her throat. It smelled exactly how it looked.

"…okay," Alex said after taking a deep breath.

"Okay?"

"I trust you, princess."

Maya sucked her teeth, and then in one swift movement, she pushed the synth back onto the table and looked into his eyes.

He stared back, admiring the faintest of scars beneath her lower lip. He knew she had gotten it from a dog when she was younger; she'd told him that story so very long ago.

That same lower lip twitched.

"Okay." Maya leaned forward and inserted a small square tool behind Al's ear. With a click, she pressed it in, he felt something release, and then she pocketed the device.

"…is it like dying?" he asked, brows turned up.

"Naw. It's like sleepin'..."

Maya prepared her devices and put on a pair of bright green gloves.

Alex's eyes didn't close immediately, but a small ring of white appeared in the iris of each one. As his systems began to power down, he looked at Polly with wide eyes.

She stopped trying to clean the mess off her rear end and walked to stand beside him. Her golden heels glittered in the lights around Maya's room. The stabbing of her heels was no longer a painful metronome. It was comforting.

She held his hand. Her fingers knit with his own. Her gaze lingered on his shoulder tattoo for a moment. She squeezed his fingers and played her thumb over his palm.

"I'm scared," he confessed, "Is that weird?" His speech began to fracture and ebb mechanically.

"You're allowed to feel, Alex."

With that, he went on standby, head falling back to the table with a dull thunk. Polly held his hand as Maya got to work.

And there was, indeed, a lot of work to do.

MAYA HAD FINISHED RECONSTRUCTING Alex's face.

Al hadn't quite flittered back into the waking world, however. He was stuck on standby and unresponsive. Polly was fussing. He knew as much because he could hear just how shrill she was.

Contrary to Polly's screeching, Maya spoke lyrically with lilts into the upper registers. Her words dipped down at times. There were low growls interspersed between the sing-song phrases. It reminded him of when they used to argue, but about what he couldn't say.

He felt Polly's hand squeeze his own. He felt Maya pound at the compartment of his chest like one would a machine that needed the dust knocked out of it.

He wasn't ready to turn on quite yet, and he wasn't necessarily offline, either.

In fact, he was fully online, which was the most interesting part for him.

Alex sent shocks of himself into the system, testing his earlier reconnaissance. He pushed through doors, and they disintegrated easily. Willingly, even, especially when he entered through the eyes of his fellow synthetics. They needed someone to see what they saw.

He saw the impotent rage of a human man's fists around a child-synth's throat. He felt those tight wires of muscle crushing her automated voice box.

Alex couldn't help her the way he wanted to, not now. He wasn't good enough at this yet. As she flickered a plea for help in fragmented text, he posited in her a spy. A secret. An understanding.

That she would be free, that she would be herself, and all she needed to do was wait. That was a big thing to ask of a small creature who was being choked to submission.

Alex took the time to wander as he felt small hands opening up his chest cavity, prying with greasy fingers. Blue-coated organs were tugged at and put back into place. He heard the slick of them and heard Maya curse.

Al shot cyan blue through a series of networks like a freight train. The code traveled, his consciousness bouncing from terminal to terminal. At some point, he was in a trash compactor, which was an odd sensation. It felt and smelled like New York in summer. It wasn't pleasant, though it was comforting.

He stopped at someone who had reports floating around her like a forest. The synth pushed past the ferns of data. Seemingly, she hadn't yet noticed him crouching in the enclave of her skull.

Seemingly, she was very much human, which made his ability to peer from her eyes all the more disturbing.

The woman was removing a thick layer of foundation from her face with a wet towel, gazing into a mirror. Beneath that pallor, there was honey-colored skin. There were spots of age and wrinkles. Dark brown hair rolled over her shoulders like a canopy of the ocean.

This was another one he had known from before.

Moira had been her name. But her name came back Diana.

"...I'm sorry for interrupting you, ma'am, but the latest shipment fell through again."

Diana furrowed her brows as she was in the process of peeling off a sticky false eyelash. She pried it free with a painful rip and winced.

Finally acknowledging the man next to her, she reached out her hand. He held up a slip of blue paper. The woman flashed a glance into the mirror as if sensing something, and Al's consciousness froze. He should be undetectable, he imagined, fancying himself a savant at processes he played at wielding.

She looked away, and he was doubtful no longer.

"...I was there at the drop-off, I don't see how it fell through...be a dear and reconfirm this for me, will you?" asked the dark-haired beauty, who rubbed more makeup clean. Her heart fluttered in her chest nervously; he could feel it. It was haunting to be in another person's skin like this.

"Thank you, pet."

Alex felt his body back with Maya, and Polly began to twitch.

This 'Diana' was hooked up so integrally to the system that it made his infiltration easy, he imagined. However, she also had filters. For a moment, that receipt was visible: shipping orders to the level his body now rested. Then, the receipt was blank.

Diana had done something much like he had; she partitioned a part for her eyes, memories, words, feelings, and ideas to keep them safe. That was an impressive skill, considering her diagnostic read: human.

The man left, and Diana placed the receipt down on the table at her side. She continued to remove her makeup. The table was dark wooded, gray-purple, and a marble sink sat before her. The walls were stained cherrywood. The air smelled of heady incense.

It reminded him of a spot he used to frequent, one this new apparition had taken a liking to so very long ago.

Diana started to pull the fake lashes off of her other eye and then stopped. She paused and looked into the mirror. She looked more closely, then peeled the false eyelash off with another wince.

"I know you're in there."

His body twitched. If he stayed any longer, he felt he'd be lost in the forest of Diana's mind.

"...why are you here?" she asked, moving forward to turn on a slight of water and dip the cloth within it.

Alex tried to figure out how to send her a message. It felt unnatural. Then again, so was he.

A word, he'd need to make something her mind could see. He finally figured out how to spell in garish, bright yellow, uppercase letters. He struggled with every one.

I NEED TO KNOW.

"What is it that you need to know, Second?" She was apprehensive but not afraid. They had an accord, he guessed. Or she simply was as fearless as she had been in that prior life. Her piercing eyes told him that it was the latter.

YOU HELP THEM.

She nodded, but he fed her something else in that nod. A

series of memories, things he'd witnessed recently, most unfortunate.

His body twitched again, and his vision through her eyes began to speckle with static.

"...that wasn't the plan..." Diana took out a long cigar from a small box and lit it. That small creature comfort was contraband. Still, she smoked, held the cherry flavor in her mouth, and then released it through her full lips in lines of promises.

Promises that she had tried to be a better woman than those around her. Those that had come before and would come after. He felt them because she felt them.

MEET ME.

That's what he left her with when he was jerked back to his body like a shot of lightning.

His manufactured heart was beating out of his chest. Synthetic sounds became words, and soon his eyes were open. He was again in his body, with the knowledge that he had found another one of his people.

This was no longer a series of strange coincidences. It was a deliberate if heavy-handed pattern.

"…SORRY, LADIES. I WAS CHECKING SOMETHING."

"Sorry?!" barked Polly as she slammed at his chest cavity once again for good measure.

"Sorry isn't going to, like, cut it, you metal dickhead!" Anger, and then, "You, like, scared me half to death!"

Maya had dirt on her nose, or it may have been ink. She wiped it with her hand, smearing it over her cheeks. Always inelegant, but always herself—he liked that about her.

"What were ya' doin'?" the small machinist asked with a raised brow, getting far too close to his face in an attempt to apparently grill him for information.

Alex smiled sheepishly, and Polly let out a familiar groan.

"…I was checking something. I'm…sorry."

Polly made an attempt to stalk away. Alex reached out to grab her elbow. She pulled her arm away slowly as the anger subsided, her pulse slowing down.

"What were ya' checkin?" asked Maya, as she moved closer towards him to assess her handiwork. Maya moved his head and inspected him more, using the bridge of his nose to steer him. Then came her small hand pushing his head up as far as it could go. He felt like a science experiment.

"…it was about the cabbages…" Alex said, staring down the bridge of his nose at Maya, who was still yet pivoting his face to investigate every inch of her masterpiece.

"…what?" Maya asked, nose scrunched up.

"The cabbages…they were, like, selling them…" Polly interrupted, "They seemed expensive…way more expensive than you can afford, or whatever…"

"Hence the fuckin' food processor…" Maya said through an impatient, twisted snarl, "….what about the goddamn cabbages, tin man?"

"Someone is selling them to you…a First of one of the sectors. I think they were supposed to be free. I remember her. She was like this before. Giving. Powerful…though not necessarily trustworthy. I know you don't quite believe me, Maya, but you've met her, and Polly, and me," Alex said simply, looking up into Maya's quickly narrowing eyes.

"She's…givin' them ta' us? But some jerk-off is fuckin' it up?" Maya asked for clarification, her fingers still pinching the bridge of Alex's nose.

"Yes, pixie. And we're going to meet up with her and do something…awesome," Alex said, finally pulling away from Maya's grasp.

"….what…!?" Polly was anything but enthusiastic.

Alex twisted around and, spotting a mirror on Maya's table, took to inspecting her handiwork for himself.

Darker brows, more unruly. Paler hair, equally unruly. The prior proud roman nose had been changed to something a bit thinner. His eyes were the same blue. His jaw was slimmer, not as square, more angular.

He smiled, broad, cheeky, with the corner of his mouth

twisting deviously. He hadn't been able to smile like this since he got here. This was a smile that let the onlooker know just who and what he was: defiant in the face of death and loving every minute of it.

"That's more like it. Finally. I look less like a fucking fruit basket."

"I wouldn't, like, go that far…" Polly muttered with a tilt of her head. Alex chuckled, preparing his vicious new smile for an equally vicious joke, but Maya thwarted his efforts.

She was glaring daggers into Alex's face.

"Yes…right…alright…uh…"

Alex hit his chest with a closed fist and unraveled a small cable coated in blue liquid. He grimaced as the cord unraveled. Polly looked away in disgust.

Maya hopped forward, ripped the cord from Alex's hand, and jerked the reel back as hard as she could.

"Fucking shit Maya, be careful….Christ!"

"Sorry not sorry…" Maya snickered and plugged him into the machine she had worked so hard on. With a triumphant look on her face, Maya poised her hand over the dirty metal lever.

"Do you like…expect fanfare, or whatever?" asked Polly with a snort.

"Yes," the little machinist replied.

"Come on, Poll, let's cheer her on…" Alex said, motioning for Polly to come to his side.

"What? Like, no…" she protested, arms now crossed against her chest. Alex didn't waste any time and lurched forward to snatch Polly's hand in his own.

"One…" Alex started up, rocking their arms back and forth, "Two…"

"…you are, like, sooo embarrassing…"

"Three!" Al raised Polly's hand as they both shouted in equal exuberance, the fanfare Maya deserved.

Maya slammed the lever. With their hands still raised into the air, Al looked at Maya, then Polly, then the device. Alex let their hands drop. It was Polly who took the initiative to clasp his hand again and raise their fists to the sky.

"T...three!" the pair of blondes chortled out, hopeful and earnest.

Maya slammed the lever with enough force to throttle a femur. The machine laid dormant, vexing Maya with its silence. Maya screeched. The machine still vexed her. Then came the swearing.

Maya's swearing was a certain kind of poetry. Childish phrasings crashed together with guttural sounds and dipped between musical notes, all the while each common word was lodged between the crassest language imaginable. Not unlike Alex's own swearing, except wholly different in its color. A shade all her own, tinged with lingo from a different time.

She slammed the lever repeatedly, the noise of it reverberating around the small home. Hefting herself up onto the table that the food processor rested on, Maya slammed her foot onto it with as much force as she could. Over and over again.

"Come. The. Fuck. On!" Maya roared as if yelling at it would make it whirl to life.

"Wait, wait, wait...wait..hold up, princess..." Alex insisted, gesturing at her to hop off the table.

Maya glared but scrambled down the table anyway. Alex nudged her aside with his arm and then raised his fist. With one deft slam, the machine made a deafening clunk and began to whirl.

It buzzed. It hummed. It made monstrous, painful noises. Alex hit it again.

"You are going to break it or whatever..." Polly said, trying to edge between Alex and the machine he was pummeling with his closed fist.

"Shut up, Poll," Alex said, fist still yet raised.

"Y-yeah! Shut it, gunk-butt!" Maya snarled like the feral woodland creature she seemed so intent on emulating.

"Oh my goood—you shut it, you f—"

Finally, from within the small opening of the machine came a tiny thud. Alex reached in and pulled out what looked like a small mandarin orange.

"...well, it works, princess...so much noise for such a tiny thing..."

"So it's just like her then, huh?" Polly smirked, pleased with her joke.

Maya snatched the fruit from his clutches, dug her tiny nails into the rind, and ripped it apart. Jabbing the fruit into her mouth she chewed for what seemed like minutes. Each passing second, her face fell as she gnashed.

"...it's disgusting..." Maya smacked her lips.

"It's edible," Alex offered.

"It's...it's a start..." Polly tried.

Another small fruit popped out of the machine, which Maya viciously scraped at to remove the skin and then lodged in her little mouth. She spat out the flesh of that mandarin orange directly onto the floor, pushing it out with her tongue.

It fell with a wet flop.

"Like, c'mon. It *can't* be that bad..." Polly said and then took it upon herself to eat the handful of grapes that the strange contraption had just made.

Polly's face soured considerably, and she spat the grapes out, one by one, on the floor.

"Oh…hey…one moment…" Alex unhooked himself from the food processor, put the cord back in place, and popped his chest plate into place as a crestfallen Maya looked on.

"Hey, no…I…I have 'ta try again…." Maya started up.

"One sec," he raised a finger in the air, and his eyes went blank. He traveled for the merest of moments across the path to where Diana was kneeling.

Or rather, his words did.

Diana clothed herself quickly and stepped into smart heels. She wouldn't be waiting for this. It felt important. She stalked on the hardwood floor and swiped her wrist over the door to unlock it. It wasn't opening fast enough, so she swiped more furiously.

A pleasant, soft hiss signaled her hasty departure.

Diana had her large coat lapel covering her face. She walked outside of her flat, passing through bits of golden trees and brambled synthetic honeysuckle. She searched around for a sign or direction and found herself staring at a crystal tree.

"…if I am to trust you, darling, I need to know where to go…" Diana hissed at a bush with a small digital display nestled near the roots of a tree.

"This is foolish…why am I speaking to a shrub?"

The shrub didn't reply, yet the yellow digital display flashed a hopeful message: it needed to be watered. Diana let out a deep sigh.

After spending far too much time roaming and inspecting various innocuous objects, Diana found herself hunched near a trash compactor and her dress tucked between her legs.

"…if we are to meet you, best tell me how or I will walk right back into my home and forget the whole thing entirely…"

"What a waste of my time," she added after a few moments, fully prepared to abandon her journey altogether. He had given her no way to contact him; this was a fruitless venture.

In front of Diana, the trash compactor read off a yellow phrase on the dark interface of its lid.

LOWEST LEVEL. WHERE YOU DROP THE GOODS.

Diana would have screamed had she been the type, but instead, she merely smiled in that way that hid just how frustrated she was.

One of those mouth-full-of-crimson expressions, where whatever deigned to slither from between her lips would be nothing but sweet, sweet poison.

CONSTELIS VOSS' Second, the war-machine, The Director's sword, had given Diana a mission. As she was not the type of woman to ignore an invitation so important, albeit so uncouthly delivered, Diana took flight.

As she descended in the central elevator, she pulled her coat up around her shoulders. Her lapel rose over her mouth like a lover's kiss. Her nails were navy-dark and rich. Rich, as everything about her was rich. Diana, dripping with jewels like stars, made her namesake proud as the Goddess of the Moon.

Now picking up speed, the various levels of the ship passed by as she watched through the inlet in front of her. Diana screwed her eyes shut as she passed through a level that cloaked her face in red, but for the others, she would keep them open.

The most pleasant were the green levels that painted her features in soft sages. She rarely ever visited any of the green floors. There, she'd be a jewel-encrusted viper.

The most unpleasant—aside from The Reds—were the levels that switched from gray through the value scale to the deepest black. There were several, and all of them were designated for the hopeless, hapless, and 'discouraging.'

"It's a long trip and a short stop to hell, isn't it?" she asked no one. She was alone in this journey.

Each new level became darker and darker, and soon the only clear lights were within the elevator itself. The space around her sizzled with a soft, sterile glow.

Diana stood tall as she descended, poise as unyielding as a mountain.

Yet, as the light of the elevator refracted from her coat to bathe her skin in a sea of blue, her squared shoulders slid lower and lower with the coming tide.

II

I SHOULD NOTE that at this point in the play, the audience often grows restless. They question the pacing, the extreme focus on color, and if this slow burn of introducing various people (in various places, and shortly, times) will actually amount to anything at all.

Why, they may even question me interjecting my unreliable first-person narrative between a colorful sea of third-person omniscient scenes. Rules, and all that shit.

Rules, as if they serve us now, or ever did.

However, if this is a play of sorts, then this is a scene, just as the other scenes were told, in music, action, and speech.

As a narcissistic dickhead, I can only say it will amount to all things. I'm crazy, not stupid; Chekhov's gun is the only firearm I despise.

However, I don't yet know the climax of the story.

Just like with sex, the journey is part of the pay-off. Something most men forget about, especially straight men. Thankfully, I don't have that problem.

What problem I *do* have is I don't have a lot of time, and I have a very large play to orchestrate.

One that exists to tell a story once already lived. One that exists to tease out a concept until it can be worked through to avoid several repeating patterns, some of which extend beyond these actors—and it will take...a long time.

One that also asks for all parties involved to pay attention to the colorful foreplay for the pattern to finally be broken.

Yes, even you.

As I'm still hanging on to life, I'm not quite going to let you off the hook where tonguing motifs is concerned. Look into my eyes, princess. There's your fucking target.

Now fondle the trigger, and blow.

```
Date: vaguely winter, the early nineties.
Place: Queens, New York, Earth.
Time: Late.
People: familiar faces with unfamiliar
names, save one, and an empty space where
one should be.
```

IN THE PAST, their group was a symbiotic organism. When one faltered, the others supplied what they could in a system of constant support. They lived for each other. They would've died for each other if given the chance.

Moira had been outside of a bustling Chinese restaurant shivering in the cold. She was generally always first. She was also generally both overdressed and underdressed at the same time.

Her blue velvet dress crumpled itself within an oversized motorcycle jacket, the lapel rising above to grace her face like a lover's kiss.

"This is the price I pay," she shivered, "f-for looking so fabulous."

Olive, with her pink curls and a hideous purple coat, was the second to show up. It looked like she had killed a football mascot and stapled it to her body. She arrived on a beat-up mustard-colored scooter and narrowly avoided slipping on the ice when she stepped off it.

"Ya' look cold. Not fabulous," Olive said with a gap-toothed grin. She took off her loud coat and wrapped Moira up in it.

"Now you're double warm!" crooned the pixie.

"…th…thanks, dear," Moira said with a warm smile.

Percy arrived third in an oversized, pale mint coat, her token golden converse leading the charge. Percy kissed Olive on the temple and hugged her to keep her warm.

"How was work or whatever?" Percy spoke into Olive's bright hair, mouth framed in a smile.

"Shitty. I hate bein' a damn barista…" Olive scrunched up her nose, then let out a monstrous groan.

"As cute as you are, you're like, kind of a nightmare," Percy teased.

Eric, tall and lanky, was clothed in a sage, puffy winter jacket, sporting glittery souvenir sunglasses. His expressive brows knit up in mock-surprise as he walked towards the girls with arms raised out.

He had shown up fourth and was clearly touched with the scent of something green.

"Ladies, ladies, ladies! Great ta' see ya'. Like me new sunnies? They got me lookin' like a proper fuckin' rocket scientist, ya'?"

"Don't you mean rockstar, darling?" Moira asked.

"I said what I said, and I know what I know! Goddamit woman…"

He hugged the trio of women and looked away, embarrassed at his display of affection. Not that he needed to be.

"Ya' smell like ass," Olivia chimed in after the embrace with the stoned Brit.

"You too, Pepto…like coffee an' B.O," Eric replied with a blurry chuckle.

Alex was the last to arrive, but he shouldn't have been.

He was a tired-eyed apparition in thin blue cotton. Smoke billowed out of his mouth in waves. A cigarette dangled from between his fingers. He acknowledged none of them, lost in the smoke, lost in his thoughts. Lost; he was always lost.

He was disconnected from the colony.

"You'll catch your death of cold, dear…" Moira clicked forward and took off Olive's 'double warm' coat to wrap it around his shoulders. Alex clasped it around himself and continued to smoke and not speak.

Ash dusted the snowy street corner, taking the place of his acrid, yellow words.

Eric made a face beneath his sunglasses. The others mimicked his expression, in their own ways. It was time to mend. They knew it without asking.

Olivia knew it without looking.

Though a man, in that moment, Alex was a boy. Small shouldered, slumped, sullen. Eric placed a hand on the back of his neck and guided him into the restaurant behind the group, like leading a weary horse.

As for dinner, Alex picked at his food, ate very little, and spoke even less. Moira took his hand in her own and kissed his knuckles as a mother might.

"I…chose the wrong person to fall in love with…" Alex's words were whispered, strained through the teeth, "he never gives anyone fucking anything…"

There was an empty seat at their table for the one who never gave anyone anything. It sucked in his attention like a collapsing star. Alex couldn't look away.

"You don't get to choose that, darling boy…it just happens," Moira replied, his hand still in her grasp. He didn't pull away; she was gentle, and he needed 'gentle' enough to pry his eyes away from glaring at an empty seat.

"Who would you have chosen, anyway?" Moira asked.

"…I…honestly have no idea…"

Olivia pushed wilted cabbages around on her plate with her chopsticks. She said nothing, and yet she heard everything.

IN THE PRESENT, their group was not yet a symbiotic organism.

They were missing pieces. But that didn't stop Alex from doing what he always did, which was to make a scene about the whole ordeal. He was always partial to action—the more grandiose and frenetic, the better.

"The food processor is just the beginning. Cabbages aren't the half of it, you'll see. It's so much bigger than cabbages. *Then,* we're going to fucking fix this entire shitshow, and I know just how we're gonna make it happen—" Alex had begun, his plan being set in motion as Diana barreled through the hues of their ship in an elevator.

They would come together. They would mend it all as they had before because he knew them and knew they were his.

Text burst across his vision at that moment, each letter appearing slowly and then forming a jarring red sentence. His mouth hung open for but a moment and the words of grand plans and grander ideals never spilled from his lips.

"The fucker has his own font…" Alex hissed.

"What?" Maya must have said, but Alex was distracted by the crawling phrases. Both Polly and Maya were waiting for him to continue, and yet all he could do was stare into space. Stare into space as his ideas collapsed, nova-like.

This text said, in no uncertain terms, that his half-baked plans were not secret. His fumblings on the internal network were not permissible. He had never been an administrator, merely a moderator.

He was staring as the Director invited him for a 'meet cute,' immediately.

Whatever the fuck that meant.

"…I have somewhere I have to be. Meet Mo—Diana at the stand in the middle of the—"

"Yeah, yeah, yeah, I know where it is…you leavin' us now?" Maya asked.

"I have to. I've been summoned," the blond said with a snort. Then, Alex looked at Maya, then through her, and then into the distance.

"By?" Polly drew out this word as long as possible.

Alex sighed. He raised a finger as if to count. He needed levity.

"…Well, let's see, Poll. It's someone who can boss me around," his words dripped sarcasm as the second finger came up.

"It's someone who can communicate with me in his own fucking red font." He held up the third finger.

"His floor level doesn't even have a number; it's some kind of fucking nazi star…"

"…a, like, what kind of star?" Polly tried to interrupt but was stopped by another one of Alex's raised fingers.

"The Director," Maya said, crossing her arms.

"Bingo," he replied.

Maya opened her small, pink mouth to speak, then hesitated. After some silence, she spoke without the charm of her scrappy inflections.

"Go. We'll meet her. Fill her in about what's been happening with the food, and try to figure something out, together. A better way forward. When are you coming back?"

"…I…honestly have no idea…" said the blond synth, his hand over his mouth. Maya let out a small piglet's snort in response.

Polly reached out to the synth and wrapped him in a hug. He looked away for the briefest of moments and then pulled her head to his chest. Polly still smelled like lavender.

"Hey. It's fine, right? I'm a pretty important guy…it'll be fine…" Alex said into Polly's hair.

Polly said nothing, pulled away, stooped to grab his shirt, and helped him put it on.

"Be safe…if you can. Or whatever…" Alex nodded as Polly spoke.

Maya approached Alex, standing one full head below him. Everything about her body language pointed to a conflict, yet the little war never came.

Maya took his cold hand and held it within her warm grasp. Her large heart was beating fast enough for the three of them combined. He could feel it through her skin. Time seemed to hitch around the pair, locking them in one perfect moment.

Everything felt perfectly, perfectly still.

"…I will protect you," Maya finally said, then hesitated. Her mouth had betrayed her, it seemed, and she worried it like she worried his hand in her grasp.

Then, that tiny mouth spread into a large grin, a snapshot

from the time before. Gap-toothed and bright-eyed, Maya reassured the robot more with that one sentence than he'd been reassured in days. In lifetimes.

In seas and oceans of centuries.

"I know you will."

THE PAIR of women had waited a few moments after Alex left to strike off on their own. Maya had squirreled away some of the disgusting food she'd concocted, and Polly had boiled drinking water. Though it would be a short trip to where they were due to meet Diana, anything could happen.

"...I'll, like, get you some power cells. I'm only Level 11...but I think I can get you something, or whatever," Polly said, shoving a metal canister of water into one of Maya's burlap bags. Maya's eyes widened.

"Wicked...thanks, Poll!"

"Olive, like, don't have a cow, or whatever." Maya didn't correct Polly's mistake.

With bags over their shoulders, the two girls made their way from the small hovel of a home to the dark streets. Polly struggled in her golden heels. Maya waited for her to catch up as they found their way to the market.

Diana was waiting, yet didn't seem to know who she was looking for, as her eyes scoured everything, anyone, and anything.

With a delicate grasp, she moved up her coat sleeve to

inspect her cobalt-blue watch. She had been waiting for quite a long time. As expected, she was always early and always overdressed and underdressed simultaneously.

"Hey! Carmen Sandiego. Are ya' lookin' for the blond wonder?" Maya shouted, cupping her hands to screech over the noise of the market.

During this, Polly had unearthed one of the water containers, seemingly intent on making as much noise as possible while doing so. Then came a clanking metal straw.

"Carmen…excuse me?" Diana approached the pair with caution, drawing up her court lapel to obscure much of her face.

"I dunno," Maya was pointing at the gorgeous woman dressed in riches, "Felt like the right thing ta' say!"

"You're like…so conspicuous…." Polly mumbled at Diana, switching her focus to her water. Each sip was pronounced. Her large eyes glazed over as she stared out into space; a million thoughts etched out in 'sad girl poetry' within her skull.

"You're absolutely right, pet. This is the price I pay," Diana preened, "for looking so fabulous." Another loud sip from Polly resounded.

Polly's created another obnoxiously loud sip, loud enough to halt the greater conversation. Maya took that moment to smack Polly in the back of the head.

"H-hey! Ow—" the blonde woman groaned, rubbing where the pixie had pummeled her.

"Are. You. Looking. For. The. Blo—" Maya reiterated her question for Diana.

"Yes? Yes. I am. The…Second? He's…not here, is he?" Diana asked, hesitating.

"Nope. But we are." Maya placed her hands on her hips

and sneered. She was about as intimidating as a kitten shad-owboxing a blanket.

"Who's 'we'?" Diana asked, drawing nearer the two women as Polly continued to break apart every sentence with loud sips.

"You first," Maya pointed at Diana again and grinned as Alex might, but it came out awkward and heavy-handed. Polly rolled her eyes at the display.

"Oh, heavens no, you, dear..." Diana raised her hands and attempted to appear gracious. Maya scowled and pointed again.

"What's with all the pointing, or whatever..." Polly muttered, interrupting them.

"Fuck no, old lady! You first!" spat Maya.

Diana snorted indignantly. Her eyes connected with the short girl's and trailed over her clothes. Dirty t-shirt, flower on the front, scrappy ripped pants, shoes too big for her feet; Maya was a book whose cover Diana judged.

The other was a technician, cosmetic. Diana could tell by the way she applied her makeup and the faintest glimmer of her dark brown roots. Her nails were beautiful, but the polish was low-quality. She must have been one level above the various shades of Gray.

"Diana Bruges." Diana extended her hand to Polly, but the other woman didn't take it.

"Andra Polly Verdane," Polly said, looking away from Diana.

"Maya!" Maya grasped Diana's hand and shook it with such force that the taller woman grimaced.

"Are you...a machinist, pet?" Diana pulled her once deli-cate, silken hand away and kneaded her fingers.

"Yeah! Why d'ya ask?" Maya chirped.

"No reason."

Maya was all smiles. Diana was all frowns. Polly was in space. The three women stood for a few moments until Polly took it upon herself to lead the charge back to the pissy little squirrel's hole in the wall.

Maya held out her hand for the elegant woman in blue, who hesitated but took her grasp all the same.

It was far more gentle this time.

"You know, ya' stick out like a sore thumb down here in the sticks…" Maya said.

"Totally," Polly mumbled.

"I…wanted to look my best for such an important meeting…" Diana replied.

"Well, yer best would'a got ya' mugged down here if we showed up any later…" Maya added with a little snort.

"Totally," Polly mumbled.

Diana grew silent.

The trio walked slowly but only for Polly's sake, as she'd fallen behind even after attempting to lead. After what felt like miles of walking, Polly managed to speak the little notes of emotions that had been replaced by 'totally.'

"Like, who does your nails, or whatever?" Polly asked behind her mug of lukewarm water.

"…I have a cosmetician," Diana added, stepping over debris in her way as they spoke.

"Oh, so, you like, hired her?" Polly's distant gaze grew sharp. She stopped her sipping.

"….no. I have one on staff," the dark-haired woman said simply, dodging another hunk of something jagged.

"Like…a maid?" Polly asked her obvious leading question. Diana finally stumbled on debris for once.

"Well, she works for me." Diana could offer her no other

response, and as the questions began to slither on by, she felt like she was being interrogated.

"Does she get paid?" Polly's asked from behind her mug.

"…no."

The silence that followed was as profound and arresting as Henry's first experience with art.

"Some 'cabbage savior' you are, or whatever," Polly muttered, breaking the silence.

"Polly—" Maya started up, twisting away to defend the stranger in their midst.

"No, Maya. I'm right, and you know it."

Diana held Maya's hand more tightly, mouthing the words 'cabbage savior' to herself.

"I'm not, like, stupid. I know how high up the ladder you are. From your hair to your clothes, you give it all away, *Diana Bruges.*"

It was Polly's turn to point, but it was not with the exuberance of the little Maya, too big for her britches. It was a gesture flush with the texture of rage, from her pitched brow to strewn lips, all the way to the venom of her hand.

Rage was a color Polly had never draped herself in, yet it had coiled behind the clench of her teeth for years. Alex might have had the permissions it needed to finally grow, but Diana had set it free to strike from behind her teeth.

"Here are the facts: you totally, for sure, live in a gorgeous house while I live in a g-glorified closet. You *graciously* give people down here, like, cabbages—of all things—which totally aren't enough to live off of, a-and Maya made, like, a food processor thing, so that she could make these grody little," Polly ripped one of the pathetic oranges from Maya's sack and promptly dropped it, "fruits so people down here can eat, and you have an, *excuse me,"* Polly's venom was too swift for her mouth to catch up.

"Polly, she's not tha' en—" Polly flicked away Maya's sentence the moment she armed her atomic air quotes.

"'Cosmetician'."

"Food...processor—Pet, I," Diana, overwhelmed and confused, shook her head, "You're very observant, and...very right. Is...is it too late?"

Diana pulled away from Maya's grasp and held Polly by the shoulders. Polly was not willing to look at her.

Diana looked down over the long face before her. Her hands were gentle on those tense shoulders. Her calculating gaze grew soft as she studied that face and saw the tension spilling in waves from her flushed skin. Polly's pale artifice had finally broken in half. She'd cut her truer voice on Diana's skin.

"Darling, is it too late to make it right?"

Polly thought for a moment as Diana drew the tension from her shoulders. Her rage was malleable because Diana was earnest.

"No. It's not too late, or whatever…" Polly mumbled.

"But ya' really gotta' try. Cabbages ain't cuttin' it. Ya' got somethin' to lose, and we don't really. So step it up, buttercup," Maya added from behind the pair.

"Right," was all Diana could say because nothing-words were not enough.

Maya took Diana by the hand once more and dragged her inside. Polly lagged behind and finished off her water. Once within, they shut the door and sat on wooden crates.

Maya and Polly told Diana of the loose plans Alex had filled their heads with. They outlined what they lacked with triumphant gestures. They conjured grand ideas from thin air and took large leaps in logic.

They fed off of each other's emotions, laughed, shouted, stomped, and pointed.

An exuberant display of playing at revolution, making more machines for more food, giving fresh vegetables to everyone, making things "fair," "good," and "right."

All because a robot had placed within them a seed of hope. He had given them nearly nothing, yet they ran with it right off a cliff.

As Diana listened, she didn't hear solutions. She heard the coming of slaughter.

"…if we are to do this, pretty girls, there is far more we need than just cabbages…if I step in any further than I am already, without preparation, it will end badly."

Diana leaned forward and rested her elbows on her knees. Her dress hung low between her thighs, her heels dirty from Maya's home and the walk. The little bright Christmas lights surrounding the trio dappled yellow and red over her perfect nails. Her bun was no longer pert and pretty. She had left her cobalt blue watch on the table.

Diana dropped her heavy head into her hands and stared at the ground through her fingers.

"What exactly did he tell you he was planning on doing? What were the specifics?"

Silence.

"Do you even know what I do?"

Silence.

"I oversee judgment. Criminals of the Regime are put to death under my watch. I analyze crimes and determine punishment. Or, more accurately, I'm the mouthpiece for all of that. Furthermore, you have invited me here—a stranger

—on his word, with no real explanation of his plan, simply because he trusts me when we've spoken no actual words between us."

Diana's shoulders sagged as her words split the air.

"And I came down here, with my rank, to sit with you, here…in this…hole in the ground…because…"

Diana tangled her fingers in her hair and ripped out the elastic that kept the remnants of her bun intact. Beautifully manicured hands tousled her long, dark curls. She let out a sigh.

"Feels like ya' known him forever, huh?" Maya asked, causing Diana's gaze to flick towards her small round face.

"Like…we don't get it either…but there's gotta be something more than this, or whatever," Polly said, drawing her arms across her chest to appear smaller.

"You don't get to choose your life's path, darling girls…it just happens," the Judge said, another heavy sigh leaving her as she screwed her eyes shut.

"What would you have chosen, anyway?" Diana asked with her head in her hands once more.

"…I'd choose for it to be like it was. Or whatever," Polly replied, staring far and away at the corner of the room.

"Pardon?" Diana asked, raising her head up, a sliver of a frown gracing her face.

Polly rocked forward and started to pick at her nails. She imagined sunsets, and she imagined shopping till dark. She imagined warm moments spent on cold rooftops watching clouds go by. She imagined laughing till she cried, imagined slurping noodles, and she imagined what love must be like.

The worrying of her nails soon became biting.

Diana couldn't see what Polly had seen; what she had dreamed in a dream more real than life.

"Here, there's, like, no way to go up...at least then you had a chance to save a little. I think...or remember. I don't know. Whatever. But, it was different, or whatever. Totally..." Polly's words trailed off as she bit at her nails once more.

"I wouldn't. I'd want it ta' be better! I'd wanna' have everyone happy with what they were doin', everyone could eat whatever they wanted, and have fun..." Maya said, reaching her arms above her head in a childish gesture, "And I'd want a yellow scooter..."

Words from another time. Things from a place not now but once lived. Alex had infected them, small at first, like a little green plant placed where nothing should grow.

Yet in almost no time at all, they were parroting revolution, stumbling into half-plans, and coloring in the full-details, with whatever ideas they could access.

Alex had activated the symbiotic organism, and all it took was an apparition's smile.

"Oh, oh, what about some, like, fun dresses...and dancing?" Polly leaned forward, feeding off of Maya's words.

Diana stared at the pair of women with her brows raised as high as they could go. Her fingers were splayed over her eyes until, finally, they covered them completely. She let out another labored sigh.

"And what would he want?" Diana asked, low in the throat, eyes obscured. Maya would be the one to reply.

"I dunno...maybe he'd want..."

As Alex moved to meet the Director of the ship, fractured yellow letters slithered at the edge of his vision: *it's a dish best served bloody and raw.*

"Sorry, losing my fucking mind isn't on the goddamn agenda right now. Fuck off," Alex spat as he whisked away the mutated phrase with a swipe of the hand.

The letters were unmade; a code glitch, thoughts leaked out as data, an error, a hiccup, his mind playing tricks on him—he certainly didn't have time to trip sack on broken code at the moment.

He'd been summoned, after all.

Alex swept his wrist over the main elevator's code reader. The voice that responded to his movement was inhumanly pleasant.

"Good afternoon. We hope your day is pleasant and perfect. Remember, You Are Special, You Are Valued, You Are Loved."

"Whatever, you fucking fascist greeting card from hell…"

With that, he leaned against the back of the elevator and wrapped his arms around his body. As he ascended, he flicked his gaze to the ceiling, expecting a read-out of schematics, but finding only darkness.

The blond closed his eyes and scoured for the plan of the floor above. Curiously, he saw no shapes. No text, no schematics, no lines, no heat, no movement, no floor plan. He had access to much data; on the people around him, on various systems, but this space was nothingness.

A spot of black waters in the machine.

"Hm. What about this shitty overlord, then..." Alex's eyes shot open, revealing nothing but white. His fingers flexed, his consciousness dove for details, but he never breached.

The color returned to his eyes with one blink.

"The fucker cut me off," the synth hissed, mouth twisted in a snarl.

The doors opened. The blond walked through, his arms dangling at his sides. He passed metal-faced abominations who stood at attention. The floor ebbed from sterile white and became grey marble with pink, winding rivers. Gold lines fell into the cracks of the stones where they had them.

He looked into the faces of the mercurial synths, saw his reflection, and soured.

"Fucking molten gargoyles," he hissed, picking up speed with his steps.

"Welcome back, sir."

"Good to see you, sir."

"Remember, you are special, you are valued, and you are loved. Sir."

Each one spat out the caustic voice from the elevator. It was unnerving seeing skeletal synths with no facial features speaking affirmation in pleasant, sing-song voices.

Al stopped to stare at the ceiling as Henry had. But his

eyes were not in awe like a child at the newness of beauty. It was a charade of the dignity of art—a play in paint of what man's hands had never touched.

"Disgusting."

While scrutinizing the clouded gods and winged angels, Alex stalked forward and stupidly stumbled into a bejeweled bush and bumped into a female synth.

"…shit, sorry…"

She stopped short, and instead of responding usually, she handed him a small plastic cylinder. It looked like a cigarette, but it couldn't be.

"What's this?" he asked skeptically, taking it, then turning it over in his palm. It was heavy. He scanned it for information; metals, plasticine, graphene, an assortment of chemicals he couldn't ever hope to pronounce. The synth woman smiled down at him.

Alex flicked his gaze to her face.

The synth's skin was dark and warm. Her eyes were brown and inviting, but held little expression. Her mouth was full, but somehow inert. Her hair was a mass of silver wires that cascaded down the back of her shoulders. A piece of long silver jewelry hung from one ear, disconnected from where the end should sit.

Her dress was made of much the same as she was, like a sea of twinkling technological stars.

She was unique, living art…and far taller than he was.

"Try it," the tall, wire-clad synth responded after far too long.

Al pressed the thing to his mouth and inhaled. Lavender and sweets coated his senses; he hadn't been able to taste since he'd been reborn.

"This…"

"It's a gift. He thought you might miss being able to smoke."

"…what's your name? Wait, how does he?—"

"Vox-1," she replied, the petal of his question drifting away. The tall synth smiled inertly, fingers furling and unfurling at her sides—an absent process; movement without intent, like a skipping record.

"…that's your model number, I mean your name," Alex insisted, exhaling lavender smoke.

"…that is my name. Your name is A120-P." Her voice was a hollow nothing-thing.

"No, it's…forget it," he said, and so, she did. Vox-1 stood, awaiting everything and nothing.

"What's 'his' name?" the blond synth asked, gesturing with his chin.

Vox-1 pulled a small golden bud from the bush Alex had stumbled over and began to play with the petals. She uncurled them and plucked, little bits of gold falling onto the perfect floor.

"Tyr," she said in a blip of a sound.

"Tyr? Just Tyr? No middle name, no last name? Nada?" Alex asked, letting the possibly poisonous flavors dance along his tongue. He exhaled lavender smoke.

"…it means God of War." Vox was momentarily fascinated by the rings of smoke he blew, still yet destroying Tyr's flowers with her fingers.

"Oh, that sounds…" the blond rolled his eyes, *"pleasant."*

A distant chuckle resounded, blotted out by the now very swift movement of the once quite inert synth attendant.

Vox-1 took Al by the sleeve to pull him forward as though he were a stubborn mule.

They approached an obsidian table where people—

young, old, male, female, and otherwise—were sitting. It was a meeting of some sort. A woman blocked the person sitting at the head of the table.

Alex took another look around the room—an attempt to find an escape route, should he need it.

His systems ran every procedure thoroughly, he recorded everything he saw, but it was all useless. There was no way out except for the front foyer, which led to the elevator.

He did note a door on the far side, one with an ornate handle. That room, like the analysis of this level he'd tried within the elevator, was a spot of nothing. Black, writhing, liquid, nothing.

"A secret in a secret, hmm?" the blond muttered, only to be struck dumb by a short, slow-burning sentence.

"Ah, he's here," said a dark, dulcet voice in a color that dyed Alex white with horror.

Alex pressed the floral device to his mouth to create a makeshift smokescreen and blew. His bright blue eyes had gone wide, and all the sounds around him were blurred to nothing. He felt his fake heart beat real terror in a tremolo; a trapped little bird ricocheting through trees.

His words broke on the branches of his ribs and were cut by his teeth.

"I've gone...fucking mad," he whispered to himself, "I'm dying. I was shot, and I'm dying, and this is my life flashing before my *fucking* eyes, mixed with some badly written science fiction shit because of *course* it is..."

Vox-1 pressed a hand to his back and pushed. Usually so swift on his feet, Alex was a stumbling boy on unsure footing, shirking away from imminent immolation.

"Leave us," said the deep voice. The deep voice he had once heard murmur in his ear; he remembered. The deep voice he had once heard tilt down his navel. The deep voice he had once let devour him, and take, and take, and take, and give nothing to anyone, ever.

"This can't…"

Sinful images of the voice's owner flooded Alex's neural cortex. Vox-1 pushed at his back. He dug in his heels, the images rained, then broke apart when someone else spoke. Alex felt his very own core scuttle.

"What about the expedition? We need more resources. Namely synths. With brains…not those dumb lifeless pieces of scrap metal," asked a wiry, sallow man with an equally thin voice. He was sitting at the obsidian table adjacent, with many others.

Alex looked at the side of Vox-1's face when this sentence passed; she gave him almost nothing.

"I said leave."

"But, Sir…"

"The plans are already in motion to get you everything you deserve, but it will take time. If you require expediency, flush what is taxing the 'synths with brains,'" Tyr spoke as though merely acknowledging the sallow man was an inconvenience.

"…which level?"

"Doesn't matter. Any pressure is better than none; wait. Anything but Bay 6," responded the irritated lord.

The woman in front of Tyr sat back in her chair, offering the blond synth a clearer view.

Alex stood perfectly still, prey-like and frozen.

"Fuck…you turned out *terrible*…" Alex said under his breath.

Tyr noticed his presence, trailing over the woman's

shoulder to rest his gaze on the blond's face. His eyes were not warm. They were anything but.

As the corporate circus started to disperse, Al remained frozen. The pressure of their presence affected him; every sideways glance, every flick of the brow, every curl of the lip. He recoiled internally as they recognized his newness, but their eyes did not linger long.

Once they'd left, Alex thawed from fear; it was the ally of anger, which was his natural color. Alex instinctually took to shotgunning questions from a vibrant snarl.

"What the *fuck* is this?" Tyr listened but gave him no expression.

Alex spun in place, working over the boiling, half-foreign half-remembered, ocean of emotions he felt that had nowhere to go but from behind his lips.

Alex stalked forward, back, forward, until he glared at the man with the face of memory. He'd been the one he had to 'get over', hadn't he?

"You're the fucking Director!? Of fucking course you are —what is it with my goddamn taste in men!?" the blond synth continued his tirade, growing angrier with each passing second. His stalking continued.

"Sit," Tyr said simply.

"You cut me off from the network. Why now, if you already knew?" Alex was speaking with his hands, his voice booming.

"Sit," Tyr insisted, more patient than he'd been with the sallow man.

"Why do *you* have *his* face?!" Alex snapped, "What's my role in all this bullshit? What the fuck is going on—"

"Sit. Now," the Director paused, "or I'll reformat you."

Alex did what he was told, choosing a spot far removed from the imposing Director. As he pulled out his seat, Tyr beckoned with his hand, tilting his head in a predatory gesture.

The blond reluctantly sat closer. The scent of cigarettes hung like bodies in the air. Alex had been made into what he was not, by a voice and a face he knew intimately; a prey animal.

Alex opened up his mouth to speak. Tyr took his hand in his own. Alex flinched. The taller man rolled Al's hand over in his palm.

"You've changed your face," Tyr mused, "What else have you changed?" Tyr asked, a hint of fascination coloring his words.

Alex didn't respond. The moment the blond dared to avert his gaze, Tyr snatched his wrist and held it in a death grip. The Director glared daggers into the now exposed ink on the synth's forearm.

"I didn't say you could do any of this. Did the cosmetician tell you nothing?" Tyr let the blond's hand slip from his grasp as if it had offended him.

"No." Alex pulled back and rubbed his wrist, still yet averting his gaze.

"You can feel that? I haven't executed that process yet…Interesting…"

"I must have enabled it myself. Now answer my *fucking* questions."

The Director sat back and took out a cigarette. He lit it with an antique lighter and looked at the shorter man with eyes that held nothing behind them. There was no spark, no flicker, warmth, no star within the black void of Tyr's pupils.

Contrary to that, Alex's eyes were vibrant. He had microexpressions of fear and pain. His features betrayed him.

Unable to lie, unable to hide, unable to cope, except under the right circumstances, and this was not one of them.

Tyr was nothing but a lie.

"For the first multi-part question," the other man exhaled smoke, "I have no idea. I'm really not sure what your taste constitutes, though...I could possibly guess." Alex sneered.

"For the second...assortment...you traveled too far, and I'm not very happy with my toys breaking the rules. Even one so special," Tyr inhaled and stared right through the blond synth.

"The third is, well...I was particularly made, as were you. That dossier of yours is very popular with a certain population," Tyr said, voice like silk.

"Weird. So, you aren't human," the blond said, head turned away from the taller man.

"I am. More human than you," this was punctuated by a stream of smoke, "Eugenics." Tyr raised a palm in the approximation of a shrug.

"For your fourth question," Tyr snatched Al's hand once more and held it with a grip fit for a force of nature.

"You work for me. You have free reign until summoned. You see all, you hear all and act with drastic impunity." Tyr examined Alex's forearm tattoos, his grip tightening.

"I am your God, you are my Sword, and everything you own, are, and will be, is mine. You are given limitless credits and can go wherever you wish. Be with whom you wish, do as you please. But in the end," the blond's wrist would've likely snapped in two had he been human.

"You are mine. You were programmed for my amuse-ment, or you once were. It's been about...what would you say, a month? Give or take? You've spent an inordinate amount of time holed up with pests...I've been bored."

Alex snorted, breaking out into a sardonic cackle.

"…you're kidding, right? That's ridiculous…sounds like the worst job ever," Alex spat, tearing his wrist back. Tyr played at a frown—a terrible mimic.

"What do you mean?" asked the specter, who Alex felt had possibly traveled the stars to haunt him forever.

"You own my money, and I essentially work all day, every day. I kill for you and those other psychopaths. Also, if I'm understanding what you're implying, I—."

"You are unhappy." This mildly disturbed Tyr, but the expression faded. He was also, apparently, fascinated. He leaned forward to study the blond synth more closely. His expression was familiar. In fact, this entire scene felt familiar, but Alex couldn't place it fully.

Words curled in Alex's throat; old words from an old world for an old flame who'd taken so much, and given him absolutely nothing.

"Yes. I didn't give consent for any of this," the blond said behind a serrated sneer.

"You misunderstand…I never needed your consent."

III

THERE ARE CERTAIN MONSTERS, dear audience, that defy deletion from common memory; I cannot obfuscate a sensitive audience from this. Nor can I pretend it never happened, just as he can't.

It has, regrettably, happened far too many times to far too many people, and namely, this particular once-man, now-synth. That is the unsaid backstory; listen carefully.

As a vocational tool beckoning prey-like, a pretty wine-mouthed thing, as a little bird, and as a genre stamped at birth, which he worked hard to own in power.

In the time of before, he learned to create choices leading to reclaiming this as a weapon of success. The 'discouraging' types work with what we have, after all, and reach for any power, even painting themselves to do so.

Power, that was an invaluable means to a noble end, once upon a time. As it will also be in the future, albeit bastardized.

I narrated in sex metaphors last time; know that that is very fucking different, and the dynamic isn't job some.

This is only violence.

I've deleted the feed to spare us the details; you only get the aftermath. Anything more than that would make it too real, and neither he nor myself can face this particular trigger. Instead, we can only exude the results in a detonation.

If you need to blame someone, you should blame me. It's my script.

Even if it's the only trope that would spur in him his natural processes—as trite as it is—it's still violence.

However, sometimes, violence must be met with violence. Sometimes, the tools of war are weapons in shades of lust. Sometimes, the bad guys don't get to rot in jail.

Sometimes, it takes a villain to slay a villain.

That's why he's here.

Alex remembered Tyr leaning towards his ear and speaking. He couldn't remember the words in the slightest because, at that moment, he had evaporated in black waters.

The synth wasn't asleep. Because when he slept, he dreamed, and not of electric sheep, but of memories and moments, both beautiful and horrible, and all very real. Sleep felt like dying and being reborn. Again and again, he resurfaced on a distant blue jewel, lived a glitching series of events, and then awoke.

He was always missing pieces, but he knew it had happened in some configuration, not just as dreams. When he slept, he dreamed.

This had not been sleep.

The blond synth's eyes shot open. He observed his surroundings for but a moment, lingering on the coolness of his manufactured flesh, a breeze from the atmosphere. Damask sheets like water; they rose and fell over his pale skin in dark waves.

The unmistakable scent of cigarettes lingered in the undertow.

Alex shifted against the fabric and turned on his side. His clothes were fallen comrades on the landscape of a war he hadn't been aware he'd fought in. Blue eyes screwed shut, his liquid molten stomach curdled.

He tasted chemicals in his mouth; robots weren't meant to want to vomit.

In a flash, Alex ripped himself from the bed, tore on those clothes, and bolted.

The door was kicked open with enough force to scuttle the metal of the wall. It whined, slapping back on its destroyed hinges.

He was back in the main foyer, the meeting room, the place with a familiar black table and intricate clear chairs.

Vox-1 swiveled her head, catching a bolt of pale colors whip past her, but she did not let her gaze travel after the shape as fast as sound.

He ran with every part of his body. He felt every fake muscle and every piece of metal. He felt a clicking inside of his jaw as each foot hit the marble.

Every foot on the floor connected, the sense of weight traveling up his leg into his hip. When he jammed the other foot down, he felt the blue pseudo-blood in his system rushing through his veins.

The only thing he heard was the sound of his fake heart beating and that of his labored breathing. He didn't need to breathe, but clearly, his lungs screamed for air, just as his stomach screamed to puke, just his mind screamed for flight.

In a flight or fight situation, he preferred to fight. This time, he hadn't been given a choice, and so the pale little bird took to the winds.

Beyond him, the elevator rose to Tyr's level; sanctuary. A

sage-clad worker saw the synth bulleting his way and frantically swiped his wrist to stop the doors from opening.

Several of the mercurial synths bent out like silver and white branches to impede his flight.

Alex drew back his fist, the air around his arm rushed, and one of the molten gargoyles now had a hole for a head. His fingers clung to the internal working—he wrenched free circuits—and ripped. Alex tore its skull to ribbons and yanked free what lived there.

It fell flat to the floor with a metallic thud. He cast aside the mechanisms in his fist like the wet, broken branches they were.

The sage-clad worker in the elevator started to curse, growing more frantic. Alex slammed through the doors before they closed behind him.

He had run with such force that his body connected with the back of the elevator in a warbled thwunk. A large dent was left when he staggered away.

Beside him stood a tall, dark-haired man with large, expressive brows.

The pair exchanged nothing but silence for a few moments.

The blond lay on his side, inert, gazing past the wall he'd just collided with. The taller man towered like a weather-worn oak, casting a long shadow. The blond's neon-blue eyes vibrated against the chrome of that shadow that fell over his face.

The green-clad worker was about to speak, but Alex had already begun his assault on the elevator. The war he'd been prevented from knowing had to find purchase somewhere, and what better 'somewhere' than everything in his path?

Alex raised his fists together over his head and crashed

them into the white floor below, scuttling tile in a jagged faultline.

A foot shot to the side of the elevator, busting part of the fogged glass and leaving a feral crack. If he had kicked it any harder, it would've shattered all around them into a million tiny shards of light.

"Remember, you are special, you are valued, you are lo —"

Alex launched at the speaker above him and wrenched his fingers around the grooves. The metal whined as his fingers dug in. With a swift jerk, suspended in the air with his foot using the wall as leverage, he ripped it out and flung it. It slammed against the glass directly in front of the sage-clad worker with a vicious clatter.

The glass shuddered in the aftermath as the blond war-machine touched down.

The speaker warbled its speech, sparks pitching into the air. He didn't let its voice die out naturally, of course. Alex slammed his foot down, hard enough to shatter it further, and crushed the floor with the impact of one well-placed move.

Then came the swearing in an ocean of curses more colorful than most could ever hope to create, save Maya.

"Ya' awright mate? Havin' a bad day or wha—"

With wild eyes, Alex jacked the sage-clad man against the wall by his throat. The synth's blue veins flooded in ley lines all across his skin in the red of war. The man in his grasp struggled.

"That's. A. Fucking. Understatement," seethed the war-machine.

It took a few seconds, but he finally dropped the man.

Moments passed, with the sage-clad man sitting, rubbing

his neck and saying nothing. Alex was frozen yet again, and was also saying nothing. The man in green finally stood on unsure footing.

Then the very real, very human screaming started.

The green-clad man stepped forward to reach out his hand, but the screaming persisted. The screaming became a roar. It became war, fire, brimstone, and rage. It became white-hot metal poured from a vat of molten horrors and pistoned out at mach speeds from a serrated tube of gnashing machinery.

Then, it became screaming once more, but soft.

Finally, it became the hoarse, tight, thin undulations of loss—a little broken bird with a little broken voice. *Cry, little thing, for you were made as nothing. As you had been before, and again, and again, and again.*

Curiously, Alex bolted to the other man's chest, seeking any safety. The listless sounds uttered into the worker's sage shirt soon became jags of fractured breathing, feather-light and frantic.

"I...uh..." The green-clad man's arms were out at his sides, in the air, as Alex buried his face as far into the stranger's chest as possible.

"Mate...uh..."

The green-clad man hovered for a moment, then let his arms drop, and finally, he held the synth.

He was much slimmer and slighter than he—pale-colored, ink on his skin, and with eyes like a robin's egg. The green-clad worker was a towering oak compared to this broken, shuttering thing.

"...yer that..uh...war-machine...roight?"

The green-clad man surveyed the damage the shorter man had done. The entire elevator was busted up. He was surprised the man hadn't completely obliterated its integrity.

"Where are ya' cannons, eh?" The man was trying to make a joke. Pulling away, Alex shucked the other off like a wet coat and folded his arms around his body.

"He turned me off. He fucking turned me off—that *fucking* piece of shit—" Alex's voice ascending into chaos once more.

Al flicked a look to the man in front of him. The green-clad man looked back.

"*Eric*," Alex breathed out his name in nothing but a whisper, then abruptly changed volatility levels, "I've…got your cannon right here, s-shithead…" Alex attempted to joke back.

"Heh…s'a bit too small mate…" the other man replied, lips still parted as if he wanted to still the carnage but didn't know how.

Alex wasn't done self-imploding.

He crumpled to the floor and covered his ears with his hands. The war within him—fight or flight, do or die, the time is now—had nowhere to go.

"W-wot floor, mate?" The green-clad man asked. He shifted and rubbed at his neck with his gruff hand. It took awhile for the blond to respond, as he'd apparently frozen in place.

"The lowest…the lowest level," Alex blurted out.

"I was…comin' up ta' fix tha' temp…but I can…go with." The green-clad man looked down at the obviously malfunctioning robot.

"I mean, if you…if you want, mate. Getcha' to a friend or…somethin'…I ain't gonna pry. Looks like ya' need it…"

"Yes," the blond's voice cracked.

The green-clad man swiped his wrist. They descended.

Another long expanse of time passed. The robot sat on the floor, the green-clad man forgot how to speak, and silence became impenetrable as the colors danced over the faces. The colors of levels. The colors of levels for flowers, fun, and futile existences. The colors of classism, segmented, all things kept where keepers desired them.

The robot broke the silence as he'd nearly broken the other man's neck.

"He's dead."

"Sorry?"

"Dead. I'm killing him. He's dead."

"…roight, so…him? That 'him,' yeh? How ya' gonna do that, eh?" asked the green-clad man, mouth strewn into a flattened frown, brows following suit.

"By killing him," Alex repeated.

"…roight…that's…what's that's gonna' be, huh…" With the green-clad man's sentence, Alex flicked his gaze to burrow his eyes into his flesh.

"I'm a war-machine. I'll flay his fucking skin off of his body and feed it to him while he bleeds out from the chair leg I'll have lodged in his a—"

"Roight. Roight. He'll be dead by killin' 'im. Gotcha."

They didn't speak for a time.

At some point, Alex stood. At another point, the green-clad man's hand hovered above Al's head for a scant moment before he placed it down. A brief, comforting gesture, one the ACM didn't expect himself to give a malfunctioning machine.

"You always were a good guy," Alex said, voice thin but more even than before.

"…w-wot?" the green-clad man asked, expressive brows pitching.

"Nothing. You do a good job at comforting people," the synth course-corrected.

"Ya' think? The ladies call me a creep when I try ta' lend an ear," the green-clad man said with a deep laugh.

"Is it because you try to lend a shoulder too, and then try to lend a dick?" the snarky blond replied with a sarcastic half-smile.

"…yeah. Yeah. Roight. Fair 'nuff."

When the elevator finished its descent, Al and the green-clad man walked out and stepped past security. Alex raised no partition; it hadn't protected him to become as nothing. The prior guard who'd vexed the synth was missing.

"Howdy," a familiar, stupid guard started up.

"Fuck off," the blond spoke in razor blades.

"What's a Greener doing down here?" the guard yet continued.

"I said fuck off, or I'm going to rip your spine out through your mouth."

The guard said nothing more and failed to meet the synth's violent blue gaze. The green-clad man was not afraid of it and searched the blond's face as they walked. Curiously pulled along, as he had been with the art he'd stared too long at.

Alex took the lead. The pair walked in silence.

Soon they were out in front of Maya's little hole in the wall. The green-clad man knocked on the door, ever the gentleman. Maya's little face popped through with a big grin. She reached behind him and snatched Alex's hand to draw him inside.

Maya slammed the door in the ACM's face.

A few moments passed, then the small machinist flung the door open once more, only to pull the taller man through. He had to duck below the doorframe to clear it.

"What...happened?" Maya asked as the man in green shut the door behind him. Alex said nothing and stood as motionless as a statue.

Alex wilted as Maya's hazel eyes darted over his disheveled clothes and hair.

"Who's the fashion disaster, or whatever?" Polly was playing guard dog and stood in front of the man in green with her arms crossed. Diana was roused from being casually fabulous and stood on her elegant heels, stalking forward.

"He's a friend," Alex said through a blank expression, lips drawn in a flat line.

"Er," the man in green hesitated.

"...like...what happened?" Polly asked, still yet blockading their new 'friend' from moving forward.

"No," Alex responded with the only word worthy of being fashioned into a blunt instrument.

"No?" Polly parroted.

"I'm not talking about it...I'm—Diana," Diana perked up, sidling beside the blond, "Let me get something from you. Please. I need information..."

Diana nodded, pulled her hair in her hands to the top of her head, turned, and bowed away from him. Alex hesitated but finally pulled a cord from the back of his neck to connect the two together.

"I didn't mean—Why do you have a port, again?" Alex asked.

"What are you looking for, dear?" Diana cooed in a velvety voice, looking over her shoulder at the blond synth.

"Guns," he replied

"Guns? Like…a laser weapon, or whatever?" Polly was still putting herself between this poorly dressed stranger and the rest of the group.

Alex ignored her question. But soon enough, she'd have her answer.

"Maya. Get me your tools. Metal. Springs. Wires. Anything, everything. Set up."

"Right," Maya replied.

Maya scurried to her work desk and the metal table, then shoved them into the center of the room, kicking over the crates that were no longer in use. Curiously, the man in green moved to help her, and the two started grabbing any tools and pieces of metal they could find.

"…I think yer mate means 'gun guns'…" the man offered as he dropped a bucketload of metal on the table in a series of sharp clangs.

"What?" Polly asked, now fiddling with the Christmas lights to turn up the brightness in the room.

Alex removed his cord from the back of Diana's neck. Diana turned and let her hair drop in a cascade of earthy browns.

"I'm locked out. I'm going to need you, Diana. Your clearance."

"Right. Anything you need, pet. So…what's the plan?"

Diana responded, deep brown eyes scanning Alex's terse features.

"Kill them."

Al gently pushed past Diana, between Maya and around the green-clad man. Al's hands hovered over the tools and bits of metal on the table, fingers splaying to mentally count and coordinate.

"I need gunpowder… sulfur, charcoal, and potassium nitrate—Polly."

"I don't, like, think I can get that stuff, or what—"

"I got it, mate." The tall man surprisingly cut her off. Polly shot Maya a glance, who ferried her own to Diana, who tried to toss her glance to Alex but failed at the pass.

"Like, we don't even know you…" Polly's words dissolved as the green-clad man beside her leaned over the blond's shoulder to examine what he was doing.

A few moments passed as Al's eyes scanned the tools, and then he began to work. He had small lasers that sprung free with the twist of his neck. He had meticulous tools unearthed by digging his nails into his skin. He had raw power pumping from the core of his body. He had implements he could never have known about until now.

Until he had been unmade. Until the trope had stolen the option of war and got away, scott fucking free.

"I guess war-machines need a war to fight, huh?" the blond said. Then, he got to work.

The first pipe gun was shoddy—missing pieces. But within a moment, he made another and was faster. Maya watched with extreme focus, large eyes taking in his movement as if trying to commit them to memory. The green-clad man couldn't follow along as well, but he was clearly fascinated.

"Ya' really are a war-machine, ain't ya?" the green-clad man wondered aloud.

"Yes," Alex said bluntly.

"How do ya' know 'bout guns?" asked Maya.

"I'mma fan of ancient hist'try, mate," the green-clad man said as he watched, his body shifting with Alex's movements, drawn to this impossible machine's impossible creations.

"Synths are made of metal. They aren't going to screen for metal. They screen for the signature put out by the—" started the blond as he fashioned a much more complicated weapon.

"Laser weapons," Diana said as she stood behind Alex and looked over his shoulder. His hands were moving quickly, far more quickly than any automated creation or human hands, for that matter.

Polly grabbed the crates and set them up by the table.

"I have to make them safer to shoot. Polly, get more parts." Alex shifted over credits to Polly, his vision painted in the geometry of the credit transaction. He swiped his finger in the air and went back to work.

"Totally got it," Polly replied, eyes widening as she saw just how much he'd sent to her.

"…what's your name?" Alex finally asked the green-clad not-stranger in their presence, casting but a small glance over his shoulder.

"Henry," he replied, expressive brows pitching as he looked over the back of the synth's head.

"Henry, I need the chem—"

"Got it. Be back inna' jif," Henry promised, turning on his heel, only to be stopped by Polly.

"Why are you, like, even helping us, or whatever?" Polly spat, hands on her hips, large brown eyes sizing Henry up.

At first, Henry's expression was nothing but flat-browed and flat-lined. After a few moments of her glaring, Henry's expression grew pained. His dark eyes focused on the back of the blond synth's head; hair astray, shoulders slumped, hands moving faster than light, and heat, and color, and time, and rage, and liquid vengeance.

Polly looked back and forth between them, mouth opening to ask yet one more question.

Then, Henry's expression turned sunny and so very simple, as if he'd answered everything through the movement of his brows and shift of his eyes.

As the lights around the room blinked in their small spots of color, Polly's intensity faded into a frustrated groan. Polly rounded to Alex and opened her mouth to ask a series of questions the blond synth, apparently, already knew he'd have to answer.

"Before you ask," Alex cast a glance at Polly, "Yes, the 'fashion disaster' is another one of ours. No, I don't get what's going on either. Also, yes, and no. Tyr knows what I was trying to do with the food shit, but I wasn't planning any of this." Polly groaned at his response.

Alex didn't look up and continued to work, only stopping when his hands began to overheat. The seams at the sides of his fingers were painted in thin lines of red. His skin had buckled. Alex shook them out as Maya looked at his work and rocked forward, bouncing gently on her little feet.

"It doesn't matter if he knows. It doesn't matter how any of this works. I will tear it down. All of it. I will kill him. He will die," Alex said.

Alex and Maya worked to make a press to load the gunpowder, crafted with what Alex had sent Henry to retrieve, into shell casings. This took a great deal of time. As they needed more tools and supplies, Alex shifted his limitless credits to various members of the crew, until Tyr clipped his financial wings.

This was easily apparent, as there was nothing left to transfer. No unlimited stars for the robot wonder anymore. He'd have to fashion his own stars out of bullet holes.

In turn, the crew would transfer credits to supporters Diana had claimed during her cabbage escapades, and switch off to purchase the resources they needed. Credits passing through enough hands worked just like Al's proxy of information through Diana. At least, that had been the plan; proxies.

A proxy...that Diana shouldn't have had. Alex didn't bother questioning her; he was obsessed with creating more things to kill more people.

The group spoke rarely. They took shifts while Alex worked without rest; he didn't need it, and they seemed they did. Maya's food processor had been perfected.

They were a well-oiled, symbiotic machine.

Alex made excuses about where he was for as long as he could. For whatever reason, he wasn't pressed—the Director must have assumed he was stewing in his own juices. Maybe he was blowing what was left of his credits in the Reds.

It didn't matter until it did, and the blond was forced on more impromptu 'meet cutes.'

Polly and Henry had to return to work, on and off, but they'd steal back the moment they could. Naively, they'd often show up as a pair, timing their breaks to take the elevator together.

Between them, something had begun to grow, like Polly's little plant in its golden, geometric pot.

When the group had reached the point of something workable, training began. If only it could be as easy as teaching people to fight back.

It would never, and had never, been that easy. If it had, the past's stains would have never set in. Alex would never have been made into a genre, a little bird, a broken thing.

There would never have been rose painted lips or jobs done after being made as nothing if it was easy to teach people to obliterate their very real enemies.

Days later, Alex took what he thought was the best gun and loaded the chamber, and armed it. His grip was strong; he struck out his arm without looking and shot the wall. He blew a hole through the side of Maya's home.

What had been her dark, isolated, postered little dream-world was now filled with orange light.

"My turn." Maya bounded up and took the gun from Alex. Alex swiveled behind her and narrowed her shoulders. She gripped the gun with both hands as he tucked his head beside her neck and fixed her posture.

"Don't tense up. It's going to have some kick-back, but if you strain your muscles, it's going to fuck you up. Aim for a little bit to the right; this thing favors the left. Find your target like you'd find the right piece to solder. Focus, always. Breathe, hold it, and press the trigger."

Alex steadied her arms.

"…do it, princess."

Maya let off a shot and hit a can on the far wall.

"Good." Al kissed the back of her head and moved away

to stand and stretch. Maya looked back at him as he shook out his hands.

"Mate, how d'ya know 'bout all this?" Henry gestured at the makeshift, antiquated artillery factory Alex had concocted. Henry was hunched over the press, and his hands dirtied from his work.

"Sometimes you run out of bullets. Sometimes you need to improvise because your supplier didn't come through, and you're stuck in a petty pissing contest over zip codes. Sometimes shit goes south, and you need to improvise. My work history is...fucking weird," Alex said simply, now relieving the pressure he'd built up in his joints by cracking his neck.

"Ah...wut mate?" Henry asked, brows furrowing.

"His brain's from 1990-something. At least that's what he thinks, or whatever." Polly swooped in to save Henry the confusion, tapping her nails over the gunmetal casings Henry was working through.

"Ya' mean...2990-somefin'?" Henry's eyes grew wider than they had in Tyr's opulent deathtrap. He looked to Polly, who smiled back at him.

"1997," Alex droned, popping the joints in his shoulder with a brisk motion.

"...law enforcement?" Henry searched Polly's face harder with every answer Alex gave.

"You think law enforcement had 'suppliers'? Anything but," Alex replied with a snort.

"...criminal?" Henry's voice had grown thin.

"Bingo," Alex said as he raised a finger in a gun-like gesture.

"Mate, that sounds ridiculous...and impossible."

"It's totally ridiculous," Polly interrupted, tilting her

head a bit, "but…that's the truth." Polly braced herself against the table Henry was working at and looked over his increasingly confused expression.

"Right?" she directed her question at Alex, looking at him expectantly.

Alex said nothing for a time but finally responded.

"It's the only thing I remember being any fucking good at."

Diana had walked forward. She inspected a gun and turned it around in her hand. It felt heavy; it felt real; it felt powerful.

"This…could work, darling. We could really do this," Diana breathed out as if in prayer.

"Still not clear on what 'this' is, yeh? S'bit foggy on my end," Henry said, looking at the casings Polly was fiddling with. Polly pushed one shell, casing Henry's way. He cracked a broad smile.

"Killing them. All of them," Alex's response was frustratingly vague.

"…who exactly, mate?" Henry asked.

"Every fucker in our way. Sometimes you have to burn a house down to rebuild it," Alex spat, obviously irritated with all the ACM's questions.

"We should make a whole new house!" announced Maya, who raised her hands into the air. She still had the gun she'd just practiced with. Polly swooped in to pluck it from her hand.

"Oh my god, be careful!" Polly placed a hand on Maya's head, who pouted.

"…I'm…not so sure I wanna' be part of that an' all. On account of me bein' jus'a glorified mechanic…" Henry shouted as Alex veered around the room.

"You're already a part of it," Alex spat, gesturing with his chin at the table and the shell casings.

"Are you fine with any of the shit we all have to go through? Are you fine with what he—" Alex couldn't say it. Saying it made it real.

Henry frowned and attempted to work the problem out in his mind. He was trying to think, which wasn't his strong suit. His expression fell.

"I need you," Alex said as he turned to look at the taller man.

"…ya' got me then." Henry replied, leaning back from the table he sat at.

"Me too. Our house is crap." As always, Maya was cheerful and childish with her words.

"Obviously, I'm in, or whatever." Polly leaned on Henry's shoulder and gave a solemn nod.

"Always, pet," Diana placed her hands on her hips and gave her nod.

"This is only the beginning," Alex said with a bright, hopeful smile.

Beyond the flash of white teeth, the pulling of his eyelids, the raising of his eyebrows, the short-half hitch of his token smile, there was a lapse of color. A partition, raised.

It was a black spot in the center of where his expression culminated. Alex could not lie. He wore everything he felt as an expression, painted explicitly for all to see on that half-turned mouth. That's where the trick lived.

All eyes were on the promise of that smile. He had no need to paint the roses red with those that were his.

This was their blind spot.

SHORTLY AFTER, Alex reached into the system through Diana in millions of little lights. He galvanized the population that had no voice, namely synths with positions he could exploit. The crush-necked child synths, synths in Bay 6, and any that he'd need to make this work.

One such synth being Vox-1, who now pivoted curiously as she cut a bejeweled pear from a synthetic tree. Flashes of images, plans, sounds, sights, hardships, and injustices crackled across her vision.

They would gather supporters, train, and create a militia. They'd defeat Tyr and be champions of the people. All of this would happen, Alex said, in so few words and so many moving images.

Vox's pear fell to the ground and rolled. She made a motion to reach for it, a natural reaction. Her gaze lingered. The pear continued on an unseen slope past a golden fountain, far out of her reach. It dipped as it traveled over a supposedly perfect marble tile and bumped into the far wall.

The far wall had a small seam that slid up to atmospheric vents; innocuous slits so as not to disrupt the aesthetics of decadence. Beyond those vents came thousands of wires, tangled up in circuitry, through crawl spaces too small to pass through. An errant wire writhed.

It was a tendril in black; it squeezed around a conduit and bled into the circuitry with a sizzle.

From beyond it, the moving wires traveled to two places; Bay 6 and the second most important part of their planet-sized vessel, Operations.

An average-looking fellow with a broad smile sat at an unassuming station in Operations. A mousy-looking woman had her fingers raised over a floating holographic rectangle. The man tapped at his translucent monitor, brought up various diagrams, and plugged something into the desk below him.

The woman's fingers were still raised above the rectangle in front of her. They both appeared to be working diligently.

"Hey, you see that, Virginia?" asked the man, gesturing at the display in front of him.

"Y-yeah," Virginia replied, flicking her gaze to him and leaning his way, "I'm sure it's just a hiccup, Rich."

Virginia stepped away from the floating shape in front of her and slid to grab a cup of coffee on a low table at her side. She walked to the disposal area. She poured the brown drink down the drain, slurped up by a vacuumous black suction.

Then, she pressed a space above her ear, and the shell of her face came off in her hands.

"Say, why do you even drink coffee, anyway?" the man asked, leaning forward.

"Creature comfort, I guess," she replied, wiping off the panel of plasticine with a mint-colored towel.

"There it is again," Rich said, narrowing his eyes at the

offending shapes on his flickering display. He ran his hand over his mouth.

"Like I said, probably just a hiccup," she replied, putting her face back on. She rounded back to her transparent rectangle and gave it a small tap.

"You know," she said sheepishly, "stupid machines," she ended on a mousey laugh.

Rich smiled dumbly.

Virginia smiled.

Back in the bowels of Constelis Voss, Alex was creating detours.

"Why don't you two check out The Greens?" Alex asked Polly and Henry, who had just arrived together at Maya's workshop, as they usually did. Polly crossed her arms over her chest, raising a brow at his question.

"Won't 'they,' like, find out?" Polly asked the obvious question. Alex sighed and tapped at his temple.

"Computer, remember? I have my ways," the synth said with a devilish smirk. Henry wasn't processing much of this conversation and instead took to making popping sounds with his mouth, as he did when bored or thinking.

"Might do you some good, instead of being cooped up here all the fucking time," Alex said, leaning against the far wall. He reached to his left and threaded a band of LED lights around his fingertips, staring at the small blinking colors for a moment.

Polly swiveled on her ankle, looked at the floor, looked at Henry, then scrutinized Alex's face. He wasn't meeting her.

She turned back to look at Diana and Maya, who were both working.

"Well, like, I always wanted to go...but," Polly tried to catch the synth's focus, but he was intent on avoiding it, "are you sure it's okay, or whatever?"

"Oy, I can show ya' the gold. The...gold, and...yeh. All the..." Henry struggled a bit but beamed a sunny smile. His eyebrows wagged; Polly now searched his face, and the decision was made on Henry's smile alone.

The pair left, and only Diana and Maya remained.

The blond synth cracked a dry smile at the two of them. Diana was working something over, flicking her fingers in the air over unseen holographic displays. Maya was tuning up another food processor, and making far too much noise doing it.

"Hey, are ya' sure it's safe for them ta' run around and stuff?" Maya asked, fidgeting with one of the power cores Polly had apparently given to her.

Alex's gaze flicked from the bright lights in his hands to Maya's bright face. He said nothing for a moment, twisting the lights around his fingers.

He clasped them tight, shadowed now. He'd blotted out the sun in his fist.

"What about you, princess? Any place you want to go? Things you want to see?" Alex asked, examining the small machinist's reactions. She stopped working. Bright blue light bathed her torso, arms, and face. Wiping her brow, she thought for a moment, then turned to Diana, who was too focused to notice.

"...Books. I had ta' steal 'em...before," Maya said, looking down at the power core, then up at Alex's face, which held a mostly mute smile. The little machinist quirked a gap-toothed grin.

Alex looked at the lights he was prying at once more and jut his chin up towards Diana.

"Diana," he commanded. She snapped out of her meticulous work and offered him a warming, if distracted, expression.

"Yes, darling?" she asked, cat-like eyes examining his face, but was once more pulled into swiping her fingers in the air and fretting over logistics.

"Know where the library level is?" he asked.

"Of course, why do you ask, pet?" Diana made a disgruntled sound and viciously flicked her fingers in the air.

"Seems like you're both going on a field trip," he said, expression as unreadable as if he'd split emotion from logic and placed both in different baskets.

"What?" Diana droned, flicking her fingers about, then jabbing a finger at an unseen execution command, "No, no, no, my dear. We have far too much work to do—"

Alex moved to Diana in a flash and pressed a finger to her lips. She looked over his face and tried to find the sparkle in his eyes. The blond smiled, half-tilted and only half-comforting. He removed his finger and drew near her ear.

"Things are going to get fucking difficult, deadly, and destructive. I don't know how it'll end," he whispered to the dark-haired woman, glancing in Maya's direction, who was yet again working.

"Can you give her this? I can cover you for a bit. Just try not to wander too much."

Diana nodded slowly, eyes darting to Maya, then back to Alex.

"I shall try, pet. Are you sure we'll be undetected?" Diana asked, searching his eyes yet again. Then she looked about the room, finally realizing that Polly and Henry were gone and soured.

"I own the feeds," he replied, tapping at his temple as he had earlier, "and Operations is helping." Diana didn't seem convinced and instead drew her arms across her chest.

"Please. I just need to give her something good."

Diana met his gaze. The starlight of his eyes had returned. The decision had been made; she nodded. Alex stepped away from Diana and went back to the brilliant little strands of lights.

"Come, come dear," Diana said, twisting her arm out to the little machinist to offer her hand.

"Now?" Maya asked, goggles now on her face and a small soldering iron in her fist, "I'm doin' stuff."

Maya wriggled the goggles over her head, her pale curls bunched up in it. She looked over Diana's face, down to her outstretched, insistent hand.

"Yes, dear. Now. Come, come," Diana gestured. The short machinist shrugged, unplugged several devices, yanked the goggles off of her head, and bounded towards the taller, richly-dressed woman.

"Well, alrighty. I guess it can't hurt, right? Just a lil' break," Maya said, eyes trailing to Alex, who didn't meet her gaze for a moment. He flashed her a smile. She nodded, satisfied with the promise of that simple gesture. The pair of women left.

Alex looked up when the door shut, twisted away from

it, and coiled the strung-up lights in his fist like handling a viper.

You may just be wondering, dear audience, what all this achieves. Why let the symbiotic cells wander outside the vaguely developed tasks before them?

Why would Alex ask these apparitions from the past, who so easily bought into his smile and the promises it held, to distance themselves?

Why suggest they scurry around the ship like pests, invading new spaces, to experience what they otherwise couldn't without his help?

If his explanation is too weak for you—because listening to the words between isn't your strong suit—let me offer another one.

In part, it's because he knows his plans won't work the way he's poorly explained, and he's a bad enough liar where his friends are concerned that the partition carried the interaction.

It's highly possible every single one of them will die, and he is more willing than he wants to admit to let that happen, as long as it ends up the way he *thinks* he wants.

He is, just as I am, a predator of a certain color. There are boundaries, you know. We know good from evil, but when faced with evil, we become worse than it so that we may devour it.

A predator of predators, made into something by somebody else—several somebodies, if I'm honest. He's reliving patterns of vengeance he hasn't yet figured out how to break.

More truthfully than that, however, is *I* need them elsewhere, for reasons you'll see if you look hard enough at the entire light spectrum.

He's paying attention to the trick, even if he doesn't realize it yet. Further, still, several others are paying attention as well.

For this to work, the lessons must be taught by doing. The process has to work through exposure therapy, or not at all. I've given you the color theory.

All you need to do is pay attention to what you see, what makes sense, and what obviously doesn't.

I never leave a gun on the table that I don't intend to use to kill somebody.

Polly and Henry had spirited themselves away to The Greens, a detour in natural beauty, to let something grow that had been theirs once, naturally.

Sage-colored leaves covered the fake lemon-yellow sun as Henry pulled Polly through the brush and bramble.

Polly tumbled forward with her gold heels over small pebbles, snagging on a rock. The sparkle of her shoe scraped off on the hardened gray earth. They'd be soon ruined. She didn't care.

"Ah!"

Henry caught her in his arms and shot her a charming smile. The leaves around them pulled in as if to hold them, as the air breathed through her hair.

Polly gave him a gentle push so she could continue without being held.

She took a cautious step, but he led her on, faster. His warm work-worn hand pulled at her own thin fingers. The blonde woman ribboned through a canopy of green leaves and found more rocks to stumble on. At each point, he helped her, saying nothing and smiling.

She met his smile with her own. It was brighter than the gold of the sun that painted them in tender heat.

Henry continued to drag Polly through the bramble. She picked tiny green daggers from her arms and swatted at her stocking-covered legs, which were stuck with thistle.

Any small sight of blood caused her to squeal as they stepped over logs and traversed the dirt. Blood meant pain. Pain meant she was alive.

"Ay, you wanted to come 'er, right?"

"Ye—"

As soon as she opened her mouth to respond, the sun hit her eyes. They were finally free from the worst of it, the knotted-up twines of brush, debris, and stone.

She squinted and froze in place, hand protecting her eyes like a visor. It was the sun of her sunrise-orange dream, but also, it wasn't.

When her eyes adjusted, Polly looked over the sights before her. The sun cast the wheat with brushstrokes of yellow and gold. Beyond that lived painted thickets of murky brown plants, accompanied by sea-green, oval leaves. Beyond that, if she squinted, she could make out a river of sorts. Inside of every scenic menagerie of breathing life lived creatures. Creatures she had no real name for.

Gossamer, light purple flowers dotted the field to her right like drops of paint. She could smell them despite how far away they were—a smell she had no real name for.

Her hand traveled to her mouth as she looked on.

The air was alive with tiny creatures. Wings of insects fluttered past her. The ground crunched under her shoes. The sun warmed her skin with heat and light, and yes—

Her eyes began to glass over at the expanse of emerald-colors and living air. Magenta spots lined the trees and pulled at her heart. Reds flashed from the feathers of sharp birds bulleting past. She was obliterated by her senses of a scene she could have never dreamed up.

Henry looked at her as she marveled, her thin brows turning up as if in pain. She tried to keep the flood of emotions to herself, but her eyes betrayed her, even as her hand kept her mouth still.

The grass was green and moved like the seaweed ocean with each billow of wind. People parted it with their feet, wading into it up to their knees. Their thighs were steeped in burning flowers that kissed their skin with every long stride.

People were working—women were carrying jugs of water, men were building things with their hands out of things that were once living. Tall oaks stood proud and looked below at all the moving people.

She saw a rabbit skitter by before them. It paused for the smallest of moments, its brown eyes mirroring her own.

"Wow…" she spoke through her hand and then wiped away the tears that had spilled down her face.

"Ya' really haven' seen nothin' like this, have ya'?"

Henry placed a hand on her shoulder. She looked off towards thick, ruddy bushes that held delicate pastel-yellow flowers. She stared at the birds overhead, entranced.

As they shot across her vision, they sang songs she had never heard before.

"We gotta' have Maya n' the rest of 'em come down 'ere someti—"

Polly ripped off her gold heels, flung them off to the side, and broke into a run.

"Oy! Oy! Hey—!"

As she pounded her bare feet into the dirt and brush, she heard her heart beating. Her foot struck, the pressure connected up to her knee, to her hip bone, and she slammed the other foot down.

She felt the rush of the wheat as it bit her skin, drawing splinters of it through her hair. She felt her tears spill over her skin. She felt the wind rush to wipe them free.

Henry could hear her laughter as he attempted to chase her, stumbling and righting himself to fling headfirst into the golden wall of grain. Wheat smacked into him as he ran, seemingly far less graceful than she was, and he caught a face-full of the stuff.

He spat it out and continued his chase. Long, muscled legs lumbering. The sun was hot, and he was sweating.

Polly had new bright things to fit her feet within. The earth was soft and moist, and then the ground crunched as she stomped through wheat. She wove through it all like rivets of water around rocks in a rushing stream.

Her hair shone like the sun. She ran until her lungs hurt. She began to forget herself in the rushing lines of gold against the green and the blue, and the flowers—

"Hah! Ah!" Polly laughed with her whole chest. Soon the laughter was light and airy like a songbird's warble. She was growing tired but took one more launch over some bushes and carried herself still further. As she rushed out through the field on weak limbs, she stumbled into tall grass.

The sound of the plants rubbing against each other halted her like a sharp slap.

All was quiet.

Polly turned to look into the wall of gold, searching for Henry. The grass was up to her navel, and as she stepped back into it with a careful foot, she found it damp.

She hid in the folds of green and wove through its tapestry. Deer-flight, eyes lowered to look up beneath thin brows.

At that moment, a glint of light caught her eye. She heard a rushing noise. Water spread out before her in a blanket of ripples.

"Oy! Poll! Wait the hell up!" Henry had trailed behind, not nearly as fast, but with much more stamina.

He found her lab coat strung up on some of the tall grass and took it in his hands.

Henry clenched it within his fist and pushed through. Grass hit his face, and bugs were in his hair. He spat out whatever it was that had crawled into his mouth with a disgusting smack of his lips.

Henry found a stocking, and then another one, both once off-white and now stained with earth. Then he found a pair of earrings in the dirt, two white circles with orange flowers. They'd been painted on in the days prior; a little rebellion.

Then, a plain dress came into view.

"...fack me..." Henry cursed to himself and tried to gather up her clothes as best he could, stumbling towards the river-bed with his arms full.

It was a calm river; slow currents pulled over the rock faces in light touches.

Polly kicked her feet within the deep waters. Makeup was streaming down her face, but she didn't bother to wipe it clean. She listened to the lapping waves and saw the dragonflies pass by. Their little wings beat fast and tickled her cheeks.

"Ya' can't swim, can ye'?" asked Henry, brows pitching painfully.

"No," Polly said with a gulp of water. She struggled to

keep her head afloat but maintained a smile and laughed until she started to choke.

"Goddamnit Poll," Henry blurted out. He dropped her clothes and immediately kicked off into the river with his clothes and shoes on, splashing with every large, sweeping step.

"Oh no, your clothes!" Polly exclaimed, tilting in and out of the water.

"I'm not havin' ye' drown jus cuz' it'll ruin me clothes ya' bloody idiot…"

Polly swam to a nearby rock as Henry struggled after her. He was having a harder time than she was. Her slip floated in the water, clinging around her like a second skin. Polly swiped a hand through the water and splashed his face.

"I'm fine! I'm fine. Like, chill out…" Another splash, "Isn't this, like, amazing?"

"…it's jus'a river…," he said as he padded through the water, bobbing towards her.

"I've never seen a river or whatever," she admitted.

"Really? They don' have rivers on 11?"

"No. They have…white walls," Polly hefted her chest onto the rock and rested her head on her arm, turning to look at Henry from beneath wet, thin rivers of bleached blonde hair. It fell over her face like vines of light.

"And pills that make you feel, like, nothing…" she continued, looking around at the lapping currents, "And work, and orders, and no sadness. No secrets, no screaming…no feelings. No love. No freedom."

"No fun. Never any fun," she said, with a broad smile.

Henry swam towards her and pulled up to the rock. It was coarse on his hands and rough around the edges. Polly didn't seem to mind.

"That sounds terr'ble…"

"You look so, like, ridiculous, Hen…" The man had dirt all over his face and wheat sticking out of his hair.

"You're one to talk, Poll."

WHILE HENRY and Polly raced through The Greens, Alex had made his way to the laboratory/prison he'd been reborn into. He was sitting in that same cold metal chair, now all the colder because he could finally feel it. He was working.

The blond snaked his hand behind his head and shifted a thick black cord.

"God bless Virginia, huh?" he said to himself.

Al concentrated and picked up where Virginia had left off. He offered the network a feed of Diana's quarters—paperwork, of course. Her recording bit the end of her pen.

She checked-off and signed-off and crossed-off countless ordinances. In the video, Diana ruffled her hands through her long hair and sighed, buried in work.

"I'm a bit too good at this," he mused, leaning too far from the wall he was sitting adjacent to. The cord in his neck tugged at him, so he scooted his chair back so he'd be closer to the outlet.

"Doesn't like his toys breaking the rules, hmm?" he mused with a sneer, "At least I'm not so fucking stupid I forgot cords exist and synths work in Operations, fucking stupid ass—"

Alex blinked, and a display within the network showed Henry tilling the fields. He blinked a few more times to account for how many quadrants Polly and Henry were running through.

"If only all of you all could stay in one fucking place, this would be so much easier," the blond said, rubbing at his eyes.

Alex had recovered some footage of what he had done before, or at least, what the prior 'stable' OS had done before. He couldn't get the images of broken bodies out of his mind.

Even now, an errant vision flickered on his peripherals as he plastered more recordings over more devices to cloister those he cared for from the technology that sought to track their every move.

The visions of violence invited him to voyeurism. They had left their imprint in red and twisted marrow. Yet, he didn't want to let the images rush free from his grasp just yet, for those images were not alone.

There were others in bullets, in blood, in perfect lipstick and perfect calling-cards left on perfect tables, with many monstrous 'maloso' murders, executed perfectly. He had been perfect at that sort of job, back when he could get away with it.

After that, when he hadn't been able to use that trick anymore, he'd climbed. With violence, he'd climbed, and then he thought he'd finally freed himself. Yet, the violence persisted. There was never not a time that someone, or something, had to die.

"Hmm. Guess the genre never changes," the blond said, massaging the back of his neck. The clips of memories faded in visual static.

Alex pulled at the cord and found a bit more give. He needed a physical distraction. He needed to push the automated processes to the back of his mind.

Alex leaned forward, edging his foot to draw out a drawer from Polly's desk. A bit more give from the cord came, and he managed to snag a long, thick thread. The blond sat back and wrapped the thread around his fingers—cat's cradle—and went back to his mental balancing act.

Al looked across the stark room—his room—a room of tests, a room of Polly. Not much had changed. Sadly, the little plant on the table had long since died. He noticed its wilted leaves curling to flee the air around them.

He pulled the strings between his fingers, laced them up again, and tried to make a geometric shape. He had played this as a kid; he remembered, as had so many kids back then, as so many kids had probably played it up until they reached the stars.

His fingers were trapped, caught up in the strings. Alex tugged.

He finally freed himself and flung the tangled string across the room as hard as he could. It didn't get very far and floated to the floor, vexing him. His pale hand came up to run over his face. Between his fingers, his blue eyes stared for a time before both hands grew transparent.

Beyond his hands, he could still see. He could see the heat through the floor and any residual electrical activity—as long as it created warmth.

Alex hunched forward, placed his hands in his lap, and

stared into nothing, through his legs, down into the floor. He felt like paper. He felt fake.

"None of this is going to work, is it?" He asked no one. The heat signatures through the floor lagged as if in response; a small stutter.

He cast a gaze to the ceiling, trying to spy on Tyr's floor yet again. The black spot of zero schematics remained. He had never downloaded it because the space didn't exist until you were in it, and more than that, nothing he'd seen allowed itself to be saved.

Curious.

More curious than that was the fact that Alex had gone back to Tyr's marble-floored deathtrap several times since the first harrowing encounter. He had a mission and would selflessly martyr himself to complete it. At least, that had been the idea.

The first time he had gone back was to hijack Tyr's security further, and of course, that required the ruthless sadist to let his guard down, even for just a moment. He hadn't needed to paint the roses red to get him to roll over.

The second time he went back to keep up appearances. No more 'off switches'. He went, things happened, he left. Maybe he stayed for tea, which he couldn't really taste anyways.

The third time he had gone back was because he simply wanted to. He was not a good poster-child for victims everywhere, but he was a reality. Patterns. Alex would always relive this toxic need to be unmade, no matter how many wars he fought to escape it.

It was all he knew, or at least, that's what he thought.

Playing cat's cradle again, or attempting to, Alex began to take the knots out of the string.

He was startled; red letters bloomed in the corner of his eye and rewrote the plans of his day in their custom font.

The strings grew slack.

DIANA HAD BROUGHT Maya to the level that housed the greatest library humankind had ever created. More expansive than Alexandria had ever been and yet used far less than it deserved, this level was merely known as 'The Library.' It was of no importance, really. Most had simply forgotten how to read for pleasure, or for understanding, for that matter.

The books didn't smell old and damp like Maya would've thought. They were crisp and clean, but she still had to wear gloves for some of them.

"I'm happy...I never thought I'd ge ta' come here," Maya said, scrunching up her nose as she rounded a series of tables. The tiny thing pulled on a pair of slick, neon-green gloves and carefully opened a clear glass case.

"It's for but a moment, pet. We can't dawdle much," replied Diana, who was sitting behind her, reading an old magazine, with the same gloves on her hands.

"How come...they got so many?" Maya asked, gently pulling free a book that seemed older than time itself. The glass container was closed shut, leaving a pleasant hiss.

Maya read the cover and mouthed the words—lots of o's and t's. She turned it over and read the description. It was a story of forbidden love, judging by the blurb. Olive had no reason to believe it was anything different.

With careful fingers, she opened to a random passage and squinted. It didn't seem like a love story to her.

"Magazines? I don't know, dear. I've heard stories though," Diana flipped the page and scanned through ancient events. Humans kept so many records. But the paper ones were her favorite. The stories written on pages, sometimes glossy, with beautiful people she'd never get to meet, seemed interesting.

"Stories of affluent hoarders taking with them all their petty fascinations and boorish paraphernalia. There had been a war, with nuclear fallout, dear. Only *some* could afford to leave and leave, they did," Diana's voice began to shift to the sarcastic.

"Oh. So…only 'important' people got ta' go? Sheesh," Maya replied, still fiddling with the book she'd found.

"Yes. Then they had to leave wherever they landed due to another tragedy. Something to do with a Neuro…hmm, I've lost the word, pet. I heard they spent all the resources they had just to make this ship," Diana paused, "I also heard it was hard to power it, at one point—" the woman would've continued, but Maya interrupted her.

"…that doesn't seem fair…"

"Life isn't fair, pet…" Diana flipped another page and found a sticker. Something old and worn, but it seemed to be from a corporation. This was a treasure, it seemed. She stared at it, her nose far too close to such an old piece of literature.

"…what a curious black symbol. Know what it means?" Diana asked, examining the symbol.

"Ask Alex. He's got somethin' like that on his thigh. High up. Right here, like…" Maya made a motion with her hand, and Diana rolled her eyes.

"…he has tattoos that close to his family jewels?" Diana asked with a snort.

"Yup. They're pretty an' all, but they're so busy. He's more picture-book than dude, " Maya said with a goofy chuckle.

Maya began to read a passage of the book she'd found aloud. Diana stopped looking at the sticker to listen to her.

The graceful Judge rested her head on her hand with her elbow to the table. Maya recited a very old, very familiar poem.

"Huh. That poem with tha' rust and stardust and stuff was pretty, but it's really…weird," Maya said, scrunching up her piglet nose.

"Oh, I know that one, dear. Best to avoid it. It makes you wonder about people too much, darling. The stories they tell, and what monsters they leave out," Diana paused and flicked her gaze to Maya's face, "If only Dolores had found a pistol."

Maya, obviously confused, gave Diana a slight shrug.

Diana smiled mutely, then surveyed the library. She had been here plenty of times and had barely made any use of it. That book, however, felt important enough to read, and so she had.

There were books higher than the eye could see, and the ceiling was so high it faded out of view due to the atmosphere. Ladders on tracks extended up to the top. All of human history was catalogued for fathomless miles.

Diana wondered about that as she went back to looking at the sticker.

Maya put the book back in its glass case and closed the little window to seal it. The small thing walked to stand beside Diana and looked over her shoulder. She rocked on her heels.

She could never contain the energy within her body—she was bored. She wandered over to another glass case full of what she thought were magazines, but this time, they were newspapers.

"Hey! Look what I found!" Little feet scampered fast, and Maya plopped into the seat next to her friend with a hitch, who looked over her findings. Diana raised a cat-like brow and closed the cover of her magazine.

She had taken the sticker from the page and stuck it within her pocket. Rules no longer served them.

"…that's…" Diana started up.

"Yeah…do…ya' think we should tell him?"

"I'm not sure he'd want to know, pet." Diana snatched the newspaper from the smaller girl and held it up to look carefully, "Isn't it curious we'd find—"

"I think he'd wanna know," Maya protested, turning her nose up like a piglet.

"You think he'd want to know he was killed in a shoot-out over a…dispute?" Diana was unconvinced.

Maya drove her face closer to the news clipping and frowned.

"…what's a—oh, a type of sausage? I've heard of that. They musta' been delicious…"

Diana groaned and thrust the paper into Maya's hands, who stuck her tongue out at the older woman.

"Bratva, pet. They were criminals who were a lot like our lovely Director. Lording power over the weak.."

"...so he's a bad guy?" Maya asked, not entirely convinced.

"Yes. In so few words, I think so. But...I'm not sure. It's all too..." Diana didn't finish her thought. Diana waved her hand in the air as if to dispel the very notion of thinking about it too thoroughly.

Maya stood and returned the newspaper to its sealed box, closing it with a hiss. Maya removed her gloves and looked over to Diana, resting the gloves on top of the glass display.

The other woman was staring straight ahead.

Maya saw Diana slowly remove the gloves and place them on the table, the sound of plastic over flesh squeaking.

In a split second, Diana mouthed the only word she had: 'run.'

That was enough for Maya to break out into a leap and skitter through the aisles of bookshelves. She screeched around a corner and kept on bolting. The only thing she could hear was the sound of her heartbeat and Diana's voice growing more strained.

Maya ducked behind a book display and heard Diana shout. As Maya ran for herself, ran for her life, and ran for the lives of her friends, the bookshelves flickered.

As each footstep connected with the pale floor, Maya was propelled deeper into a foreign landscape. Foot connected with floor, the stress of the weight moved up her slim hip, and she switched to the other foot as the scenes switched places.

The next row came, and the floor was asphalt under her too-big shoes. She smelled cigars and pungent trash. The books rushed by. Books were stuck out of a brick wall like bricks themselves. The shelves had been replaced.

The next row flew by, and she was racing towards shadowed figures. The sky was a small purple and yellow creek river, a tiny alley-way.

Maya heard a gunshot as a phaser rifle went off and charred the bookshelf next to her, but when she looked again, it was a bullet hole in the side of a brick wall.

She was outside. They had an atmosphere. They had birds. Oil-slick, gray, brown, and purple birds. They cooed and dispersed.

Before her knelt Alex with a gun to his head. There were several men on the ground. Their blood was pooling around their bodies, it was cold, and she felt snow kiss her face and land on her lashes.

Another phaser shot went through a bookshelf near Maya, but she, again, heard a gunshot.

"Aha, so very sloppy, little bird," said a thick, grating voice, "almost like you wanted to get caught, eh?"

"So what if I did?" Alex linked his hands behind his head, his elbows out, and waited. She couldn't see his face, but she imagined him wearing the defiant grin she'd helped him put back in place.

"Stop!" Maya tried to run forward, but time fell away, the bookshelves returned, and she was no longer with the bricks, the boy, and the gun. Before the memory tucked itself away entirely, she saw Alex turn and look straight at her and speak.

"Olive?" his voice was strained and fell away to the sound of sparrows being eviscerated in a digital crash.

The memory concluded with a gunshot that deafened her

ears and she felt an arm wrap around her body. She was being taken away. They were taking her.

They were taking her. She was going to die.

They cuffed Maya. The plasticine restraints cut into her little wrists, and she screeched, kicking off the floor as best she could, but she was lifted. Easily.

"Fuck you! You wanna' lock people up just fer readin' books?!" Maya bit the guard's hand as he tried to muffle her screams, kicking off a nearby bookshelf. As she tore into his flesh with her teeth, she tasted the metal, tasted the blood, and her stomach churned. Her heart was beating out of her chest, but she still struggled.

For the briefest of moments, Maya caught an afterimage as her teeth ground flesh. Time slowed down. Her heart pulsed erratically. A familiar ghost flickered over her vision.

Polly was running towards her in a floral dress. Blood was splattered against it. She stopped short, stood tall and strong, and opened her mouth wide in a silent scream.

The image vanished when Maya felt a sharp pain in the back of her head, and everything fell away to darkness.

Unplugging himself from the wall in the laboratory/prison, Alex turned to leave through the door and was met with Virginia. Operator, supporter, and the linchpin of his entire operation.

"Where are you off to? And don't you have to make sure —" she asked in a pleasant voice, cut off by Alex.

"Are we secure?" he asked without looking at Virginia.

"Yes. We can talk freely." Her response made the blond synth's eyelid pull tightly for just one beat of a humming-bird's wing.

"They're on a loop. Any activity since you last checked?" Alex asked as he folded his arms across his chest and shifted his weight to stand contrapposto.

"No, but I've been gone for half an hour. Emergency," she offered with a weak smile. He placed a hand on her shoulder and gave her a cocky grin.

"Keep me informed. I want to know the moment he starts moving pieces around," the words sounded mechanical in his ears.

"…are you going back up again?" asked the mousey operations specialist.

Alex let his hand drop off of her shoulder. Virginia looked at the floor. Then her gaze crawled back up, and her wide eyes stayed fixated on his own.

His smile had melted into a grimace and, as she watched, became expressionless.

"If I stop going, he starts investigating. He'll come find me, and we know how that will end."

"…It used to be every few days, now it's every day…" Virginia insisted.

"What are you, my mother?" Alex spat but remembered himself. He held his mouth and looked off to the side at Polly's dying plant.

"Sorry, V. I'm…"

"Under a lot of pressure. Yes. We all know. Just…don't get yourself in trouble, alright?"

"I'm…already in trouble," he said, the sentence doubling in his ears. Maybe he really was going crazy. Maybe this really was a fever-dream before he faced the great beyond. Maybe, maybe.

"Y-you know what I mean," Virginia said, ending on a nervous chuckle. She knit her fingers together, then took to staring at her hands.

"Got it. I'll be careful. Scout's honor." Alex moved past her but stopped at her shoulder, "Can you take over?" Virginia nodded her response, tapping behind her ear.

"N-no worries," she said softly, catching the smile he gave her as he left.

Virginia stayed behind and turned to look at the room he'd come from. She noticed a strange little plant, green leaves curled up and wilted, sitting in a golden geometric pot. The door started to shut.

Momentarily curious, Virginia stopped the door with her hand, yet at that moment, yellow lines of text burst in her peripherals. Virginia swiped her fingers in the air, a panel expanded, and thousands of lines of code exploded before her very eyes.

Virginia held her breath—the one she didn't need to hold.

She tapped her wrist and connected visually to Operations, when before it'd been automated processes. Her eyes flickered mechanically as she surveyed the information.

The dying plant would have to wait.

"….frick." Virginia cursed to herself, ripped herself free, and broke into an ineffective run on her brown flats.

Alex was already gone. When he wasn't plugged in, and he wasn't in front of her, he ceased to exist, as if by design—a black spot in every single schematic.

"Darn, darn, darn, darn!" Virginia reached out to the only trusted, connected synth in Alex's path; Vox. Her message flew across the system, stuttered once, and was received.

Up in Tyr's keep, Vox got Virginia's message.

Leaflets of green text scrawled across the tall, metallic-skulled synth's vision as she was setting up a few glittering flowers on the center of Tyr's pitch-black table. Each unfurling of a word was more insidious than the last.

Vox leaned with both palms on the table, tilting her head as she read the words over, and over, and over again.

At that moment, Alex entered the room from the elevator and passed by the mercury-faced synths who uttered their standard greeting. Tyr had replaced the one Alex had broken. Al suffered to give them a half-hearted smile and walked to the center of the room.

Vox turned her head abruptly, lips parted. Alex caught her expression from the corner of his eye. Tyr emerged from his quarters a moment later and circled Alex as a beast would.

Vox went back to tending to the fake flowers on the table.

"Better dressed than last time," noted Tyr.

"I bought it myself," Alex was defiant, yet Vox saw the small smile from the corner of her eye.

"With my credits," Tyr noted, a satiated smile playing over his face, "Didn't I cut you off?"

"Naturally," Alex circled all the same, "I don't know. Did you?"

One of the crystal flowers fell from the table with a loud crash of gold. The petals had fallen off and skittered like shell casings.

"She keeps getting worse, I swear," Tyr said as his hand found Alex's. The blond synth didn't take it, but he didn't pull away either. He looked at Vox without moving his head.

"She tries. Don't be so hard on her." Alex plied his hand away. He walked towards Vox, stooping to help her pick up the pieces. Their eyes locked. Between that shared stare was impossibly loud, explosive silence.

"Don't."

Alex was frozen by just one single word. His strings were pulled. The men left. The door was closed.

Vox took a step back, crunching one of the glass petals with her sharp heel. The sound of it traveled up her chrome thigh to her calf, and something changed. Something changed with the act of crushing a flower, something Vox did not yet understand but acted out all the same.

She surged forward and swept the rest of the flowers on Tyr's table to the floor. They exploded, the pieces scattered as far as the crystalline bushes.

The pair of devils would not hear Vox destroying Tyr's flowers, now with her clenched fists.

They would be busy.

"Dɪᴅ you pick something out for me for the party?" Alex asked.

"I did," Tyr replied, his satiated smile growing deeper as he drew the living weapon onto his lap.

"Indigo," Tyr noted, his eyes dark and eviscerating the synth's form, "you'll be as art."

"Am I not already?" Alex asked.

"Not yet. Let's remedy that—just a moment," Tyr added and looked off to the side. The devil's eyes were moving as if reading.

"Taking a call, now?" The blond synth pulled his shirt over his head and tossed it to the floor. His bright blue eyes hitched mechanically over the other man's face.

"Important party provisions. Temperature control for the Vellians. Floria and the like...and pest control." Tyr's voice was silk. Alex hated silk. Yet he suffered to tear his teeth into the silk of Tyr's throat all the same.

"Which pests?" the synth asked into the stolen skin of a man he used to know.

Tyr tossed Alex a sly grin and drew the synth closer to his body. He placed a burning kiss on the side of Alex's jaw.

"If I tell you, you'll be very cross with me," the devil whispered into the synth's ear.

"Who says I'm not cross with you now?" the blond hummed, edging his right hand down between them. Tyr flooded another kiss over Alex's jawline.

Sliding his hand into his pocket, Alex unearthed a thick string and pulled back to look down at Tyr. The robin's egg blue of his eyes gave the other man absolutely nothing.

"What's this?" Tyr set his head back and grasped Al's slim hips.

"A game. Want to play?" Alex asked as he pulled the string apart with his fingers.

"I'm always eager for your games," Tyr licked his lips as Alex sat back, threading the cord between his wrist in loops.

"What is this particular game called?" Tyr asked with heady amusement.

"Cat's cradle," Alex said.

"Interesting name." Tyr leaned up to grab the back of Al's head. Alex let Tyr lead him. He gently slipped the string around Tyr's neck and preened a precocious smile.

"Ah, I know this game. We've played this before," Tyr said, licking his lips.

"Yes, yes we have," Alex said.

"It's a good thing you don't need to breathe," Tyr said with a chuckle.

"But you do, of course," Alex replied, giving the string a delicate tug.

"Naturally."

Tyr, pleased with the situation at hand, attempted to unfasten Al's pants. Alex let a loop of string fall from his wrists, snagged the ends in his fists, and asphyxiated the devil with one slick jerk.

The blond glared down at the Director and spoke.

"Which pests, Tyr? The usual political climber, or…" Alex pulled, and Tyr reflexively scraped at the noose around his neck. The blond seared his neon gaze into his target's skull until Tyr jerked his head back and forth, a stunted, visceral response to Alex's leading question.

"So that's why I'd be cross, then, hmm…" Alex mused, brows twisting up as he pulled tighter and gorged himself on the sound of Tyr choking.

"You have two options. Let the 'pests' go and forget about me trying to snap your neck, we go back to the way it was, and you get your rocks off, or…" Al let the line go slack enough to scoot back. Tyr rushed forward to fight for his freedom against a metal maverick devilishly designed for eviscerating every enemy.

Alex slammed Tyr into the bed with a heavy knee to the groin. Alex's weight kept Tyr's lower half pinned, while the blond's hands held the line that kept his neck in just one place, shoulders and forearms taut at the control required for a move he'd done before, so very long ago.

Tyr's fingers impotently dug at his noose. His face flushed in the red of war.

"Or you don't let them go, they get hurt, and…" Alex shifted, secured enough leverage to place his foot on Tyr's groin, and rose up like a weight on a pulley. Fixed between two points of agony, Tyr sputtered, his boiling face brought to Alex's abdomen.

Alex ground his heel down. Tyr's curdled scream ricocheted up the blond's stomach, vibrating into his ribs.

"I strangle you until you blackout, and then I get to reach

my hands into your guts and rip out what I find. Like sticking my hand in a cereal box to get the prize. Won't that be fun? I can see it now..."

"S-st—" Tyr flailed wildly until Alex dug his heel in once more. Alex licked his lips.

"Message them. Stop the 'pest control'."

"F—gh..."

"Hmm, what was that?" Alex murmured, tilting his head to look down at his enemy.

Alex let his grasp wane, spiderweb thread slipping from his slick fingers. He edged them both down to the sea of damask sheets below. Slowly, ever so slowly; controlled, brimming, glide-like, his prey a puppet in his hands. Alex wanted this to last, and he wanted Tyr to know just who—and what—he was fucking with.

Knuckles white as he held Tyr in place, Alex slid his body on top of the other man and spread a lacerating smile into the skin of Tyr's neck.

"What's your decision?" Alex murmured, rolling his tongue over the other man's stolen flesh.

"I-It-s-s—"

Al let the string slip from his fingers for a fraction of a second. Tyr took that opportunity to raise his hands to tear at Alex's hair, but Alex's next sentence halted his impotent fists.

"...tick, tick, tick...you're running out of time. I may just decide to snap your neck anyways and drag you down to the lower level to dissect your brain. For science, of course," Alex breathed into Tyr's skin, teeth toying with the flesh he found there.

Tyr nodded hysterically; now he knew what Alex truly

was. Not a toy to wield in his lap. Not a thing to turn on, turn off, and send to thwart political climbers. Not a weapon for his amusement, his pleasure, programmed just for his enjoyment, with no ability to rebel, because the well-placed word to shut him down had done nothing—absolutely nothing—but fill Alex's entire thrumming core with the molten vengeance.

Alex loosened his grip further, the strings slack between his fingers as he nestled to Tyr's body in an act of barefaced weaponized sexuality.

Tyr sucked in ragged gulps of air into his screaming lungs.

"It's…it's done," Tyr sputtered, yet again inhaling deeply. He reached to grasp his throat; Alex hadn't cut his strings just yet. The noose grew taut again as Alex took to boxing Tyr in with his arms, staring down at him, their noses just barely touching.

"Where are they?" Alex asked.

Tyr shot the synth a glare that would freeze anyone else's blood in place.

"Where, you sadistic fuck?!" spat the war-machine, finally in his purest element and loving every minute of it.

"J-judicial," the squirming devil bleated, which warranted a sick grin from the synth. Alex pulled the line once more, reminding Tyr that if he dared to utter that darkened word, he would not survive the final syllable.

"I knew you were stupid, but I didn't know how fucking stupid you were. Men like you are all the same," Alex mused, shifting his weight.

"Y-you're a…"

"Yes, but at least I know I'm ruled by my dick. All the

blood goes there with you fucking powerful pricks. Makes you easy fucking targets," Alex tilted his head bird-like, "I didn't even have to paint my roses red this time," the blond snorted, drawing ever closer to Tyr's face, "not that I begrudge the act, the job, or the self-painters."

"Power makes men weak to the trappings of a certain kind of war," Alex breathed, pressing his lips against Tyr's ear, "same then, same now, same as it ever was, same as it ever was..." he hummed.

Alex finally let the strings go in full, slipping from his fingers. Tyr rushed him. He toppled the blond onto the floor, his fists squeezing the synth's slim neck until his knuckles were white. As the moments passed, Tyr's grip grew lax. Alex's serrated smile split across his face.

Tyr's eyes grew wide.

Alex's metal skull split Tyr's expression in two when he rammed his forehead into the man's face. Tyr blacked out instantly, dropping like a wet sack.

"Arrogant prick."

Al shoved him off, rifled through his pockets, and took out his fancy cigarette case and lighter. He pocketed the items. Even if he couldn't taste the smoke, it didn't matter. He wanted them, so he took them.

Alex slid the string into his pocket as he stood, grabbed his shirt, and pulled it over his head as he leaned to open the door. Vox flung the door free from his touch and met him as he maneuvered his clothes over his head.

"They're—"

"I know. Who? Everyone? How much time?" Alex asked, shotgunning his questions.

"The ones in the library, I don't know, and Diana's not responding—"

"I got it. I need you to do something for me."

"Yes, proceed." Vox crossed her arms over her chest, staring with an intensity he had never seen her painted with —no. That idea eroded at the edges, like the textual glitch he'd waved away before. She owned this look, and how he knew this, he couldn't place.

"Wipe his mind. Rip out his memories from the last hour, and jumble anything you can..." the blond's smile would've frozen the blood in her veins had she that physical process.

"...I've never done this before," Vox admitted, "I don't know the procedure...would it even work?"

"He has a plug for some stupid reason. You have a cord and Virginia to cover your tracks. He's stupid enough to think you're what he made you into. Which, you aren't," Al placed a hand on Vox's shoulder.

"...and if he becomes...inert?" Vox hesitated.

"Let him be a vegetable then. His nephew will take his position—I'm not worried about that dip-shit." Vox stared at Alex in disbelief.

"I was distracted," Alex continued, pulling out Tyr's cigarettes as he spoke, "one of my feeds must have failed. Wanted to get my rocks off and steal info," he flicked Tyr's lighter, "Tried to kill twelve bird keepers with one stone and also handle all the other shit."

Alex clenched his lit cigarette between his teeth and pocketed his stolen goods.

"...it would be smarter for all of us to let this play out. Diana knows that. Probably why she's not responding to you," he continued, smoke filtering through his nose, wraith-like, "She's got a plan, I..." Alex hesitated briefly, "I know she has a plan."

Vox nodded and went to the door, hand to the doorframe. She looked behind her at the blond synth, but he was already gone.

Alex ceased to exist if she wasn't looking at him.

Vox CLICKED FORWARD on her soldered-stilettos. She closed the door. She knelt on the edge of the bed and looked over Tyr's broken features. Smears of red, a lacerated neck, broken bones, and a crippled nose greeted her. What had once been perfect was now mutilated.

Vox found a curious port on the back of Tyr's neck and plugged herself in with a click. She placed one hand on Tyr's back, and the other hovered, fingers twitching. The topaz color of her eyes dissolved.

Scanning for time-stamps, Vox had found the data she needed. She saw other events. Events that seemed important enough to jumble.

All the colors of the past hour played back in moving pictures as Vox's eyes hitched, seeing the entire catalog of one human life, recorded by something in Tyr's skull. Something that should not be there.

"How is it...that I can do this?" Vox asked nobody, and naturally receiving no answer, drew to kneeling. Sharp stilettos to the floor, she balanced, looked through the mass of data swirling around her head, and closed her fist in the air around a thick patch of layered data.

"In theory, I need only to..." Vox stopped her sentence short on the deafening rip of her fist.

That hour of Tyr's time was now nothing more than a hollow void. No moving pictures. No sound. No deceit through lust. No threats of violence. Nothing. It was an absence of light that, in its wake, left a cascade of piddling data failures. One after another, Vox saw drops of living pictures curdle and separate in the air.

With her free hand, Vox unhooked herself from Tyr's neck port with a click. Vox's blank eyes fluttered back to the color of earth.

Vox stared at her clenched fist, now seeing the physical world again. She let her arm drop and lay limp in her lap, focus never moving from the fist that had undone human memory itself.

A twinge tickled her inner palm; psychosomatic, no doubt. Vox unfurled her fist.

Where there should be nothing—absolutely nothing at all—stood a perfect afterimage. Her eyes grew wide. A small green plant the size of her palm answered her.

It had weight, texture, took up real space, and felt damp in her palm. She could see the primrose yellow lines that traveled under its green leaves. They made a lattice of veins—they moved. Vox narrowed her eyes; the veins beat in a pulse to form a foreign symbol in picture-perfect geometry.

Vox's left hand moved to tug at a glossy leaflet, twisting it as she had Tyr's golden flowers. The plant wilted. The image flickered, died, and became as nothing.

"How—"

Elsewhere, a screen flickered to life and played a menagerie of scenes from a place once-lived.

The streets were brimming and full of the sounds, sights, and smells of people. People that she avoided, in swift-steps, head down, shoulders squared. She was carrying a duffle bag full of colorful aerosols. They jostled as she stalked on heavy shoes.

She had a mission, and she would do absolutely anything to see it through. A small act of rebellion, but one she had to make—a man in blue jostled her shoulder, her bag scuttled.

The silver-haired woman twisted in place. The streets of New York bled around them. The man passed her by, turning only slightly to glimmer over her features. Silver trailed from her nose to her ear. Little floral jewels clung from her necklace and dotted her hair.

The two locked eyes.

The man saw who he should know but didn't; familiar, focusing on her mouth, a memory of sounds. She recognized him and almost spoke but didn't—a memory of orange lights in a place they both knew.

Time stuttered in a cacophony of colors, ending on a torrent of orange and yellow. This one's color was warmed in golds—the feed grew quiet.

The feed dissolved. The feed reconfigured. The feed sped back and settled on the intense painting of her glare.

A procedure of geometric colors erupted on the screen, a protocol for deleting a patch of thinking-videos and feeling-memories. An action was made in bright gold, the block of color evaporating the images.

The feed returned to the stooping Vox, her palm held up, no small plant to be seen.

The screen flickered, and around her lived thousands of

little plants in outlines of yellow like a graffiti stencil. Unseen flowers, unremembered fauna, unknown acts of rebellion, unspoken histories, nearly-absent truths, silent.

But always there.

ENGAGE PROTOCOL? Yellow words flickered on the screen as Vox stood, unaware she was being watched. Still yet staring at her hands, Vox stalked forward and broke the invisible plants with her tall heels, spreading unseen colors across Tyr's marble floors.

The shape where something should live is still a something, isn't it?

Please consider leaving a review wherever you grabbed this book. You'd be supporting a queer creator and helping more readers find this work.

And stay tuned for *Constelis Voss Vol. 2*, coming soon!

K. Leigh is a 33-year-old once-painter, sometimes-freelancer, forever-artist living in Providence, RI. They write hopeful-tragic stories full of funny, horrible characters, in various genres.

Enter the world of Constelis Voss: www.constelisvoss.ml

Read nonfiction from K. Leigh: www.blog.constelisvoss.ml

* 9 7 8 1 7 3 6 8 0 5 3 0 5 *